Elizabeth Ferrars and The Murder Room

››› This title is part of The Murder Room, our series dedicated to making available out-of-print or hard-to-find titles by classic crime writers.

Crime fiction has always held up a mirror to society. The Victorians were fascinated by sensational murder and the emerging science of detection; now we are obsessed with the forensic detail of violent death. And no other genre has so captivated and enthralled readers.

Vast troves of classic crime writing have for a long time been unavailable to all but the most dedicated frequenters of second-hand bookshops. The advent of digital publishing means that we are now able to bring you the backlists of a huge range of titles by classic and contemporary crime writers, some of which have been out of print for decades.

From the genteel amateur private eyes of the Golden Age and the femmes fatales of pulp fiction, to the morally ambiguous hard-boiled detectives of mid twentieth-century America and their descendants who walk our twenty-first century streets, The Murder Room has it all. **›››**

The Murder Room
Where Criminal Minds Meet

themurderroom.com

Elizabeth Ferrars (1907–1995)

One of the most distinguished crime writers of her generation, Elizabeth Ferrars was born Morna Doris MacTaggart in Rangoon and came to Britain at the age of six. She was a pupil at Bedales school between 1918 and 1924, studied journalism at London University and published her first crime novel, *Give a Corpse a Bad Name*, in 1940, the year that she met her second husband, academic Robert Brown. Highly praised by critics, her brand of intelligent, gripping mysteries was also beloved by readers. She wrote over seventy novels and was also published (as E. X. Ferrars) in the States, where she was equally popular. *Ellery Queen Mystery Magazine* described her as 'the writer who may be the closest of all to Christie in style, plotting and general milieu', and the *Washington Post* called her 'a consummate professional in clever plotting, characterization and atmosphere'. She was a founding member of the Crime Writers Association, who, in the early 1980s, gave her a lifetime achievement award.

By Elizabeth Ferrars
(published in The Murder Room)

Toby Dyke
Murder of a Suicide (1941)
   aka *Death in Botanist's Bay*

Police Chief Raposo
Skeleton Staff (1969)
Witness Before the Fact (1979)

Superintendent Ditteridge
A Stranger and Afraid (1971)
Breath of Suspicion (1972)
Alive and Dead (1974)

Virginia Freer
Last Will and Testament (1978)
Frog in the Throat (1980)
I Met Murder (1985)
Beware of the Dog (1992)

Andrew Basnett
The Crime and the Crystal (1985)
The Other Devil's Name (1986)
A Murder Too Many (1988)
A Hobby of Murder (1994)
A Choice of Evils (1995)

Other novels
The Clock That Wouldn't
   Stop (1952)

Murder in Time (1953)
The Lying Voices (1954)
Enough to Kill a Horse (1955)
Murder Moves In (1956)
   aka *Kill or Cure*
We Haven't Seen Her Lately
   (1956)
   aka *Always Say Die*
Furnished for Murder (1957)
Unreasonable Doubt (1958)
   aka *Count the Cost*
Fear the Light (1960)
The Sleeping Dogs (1960)
The Doubly Dead (1963)
A Legal Fiction (1964)
   aka *The Decayed Gentlewoman*
Ninth Life (1965)
No Peace for the Wicked (1966)
The Swaying Pillars (1968)
Hanged Man's House (1974)
The Cup and the Lip (1975)
Experiment with Death (1981)
Skeleton in Search of a
   Cupboard (1982)
Seeing is Believing (1994)
A Thief in the Night (1995)

Murder Moves In

Elizabeth Ferrars

HEADLINE BOOK PUBLISHING
A division of Hodder Headline PLC
338 Euston Road
London NW1 3BH

An Orion book

Copyright © Peter MacTaggart 1956

The right of Elizabeth Ferrars to be identified as the author of this work has
been asserted in accordance with the Copyright, Designs and Patents Act 1988.

This edition published by
The Orion Publishing Group Ltd
Orion House
5 Upper St Martin's Lane
London WC2H 9EA

An Hachette UK company
A CIP catalogue record for this book is available from the British Library

ISBN 978 1 4719 0700 5

www.orionbooks.co.uk

CHAPTER 1

Waiting at the crossroads while a lorry with a trailer, two cars, a bus and a man on a bicycle went by on the main road to Blanebury, Douglas Birch saw the lights in the Mellanbys' house. He looked at them abstractedly, as abstractedly as he answered the good evening called out to him by the man on the bicycle. Only when he started to cross the road, it occurred to him to wonder who the man might have been, and why there should be lights in that house that evening.

There were lights in most of the windows.

Douglas frowned and the frown made his dark, round face with the soft mouth and prominent, dreamy eyes look peevish. A not very urgent sense of responsibility told him that he probably had a duty to go in and discover the reason for the lights. But the thought of this interfered with his concentration on the only subject that was capable of interesting him at present. For the last hour, on the walk that he took every afternoon after writing three thousand words of his novel, he had brooded on this one subject, deriving a bitter pleasure at being able to turn his whole mind to exploration of the pain it caused him.

But now there were lights in the Mellanbys' house.

The problem of why they were there jerked his mind off its single track of suffering, sending it resentfully asprawl among practical matters.

He walked on slowly, thinking that since there was no one to see him in the dusk he might easily walk straight on. He was a man of medium height, broad-shouldered, but with a soft and sedentary look about him, though his skin was deeply tanned showing that he spent much time in the open air. He was forty-one but looked older, except for an

1

unchanging childishness in his expression. His dark hair had grown thin and, with the November wind blowing it about, had fallen in wisps about his ears. There was a roll of flesh above his collar. He was wearing an old tweed suit and heavy walking shoes.

The Mellanbys' house was about fifty yards down the road, on the right. It was a small stone house, standing in a neglected orchard, enclosed by a low, dry stone wall. The wall had been broken down in places and dead stalks of nettles and cow parsley stood tall in the grass between the leafless fruit trees. On the window frames and doors of the house the paint was blistered and peeling.

Reluctantly Douglas turned in at the gate, crossed the small, paved court to the entrance and rang the bell.

From inside he at once heard squeals of excitement, followed by a woman's voice demanding instant quiet, then quick steps came to the door and it was opened by Robina Mellanby.

She was a small, thin woman of thirty-three, with a thin, sharply pointed face in which the rather sombre grey eyes, with unusually long lashes, were the only arresting feature. She was dressed in jeans, a loose sweater and soiled white canvas shoes. Her brown hair was scraped off her face and tied back in a horse's tail with a yellow ribbon. There was a black smudge down one of her cheeks. Some fragments of straw were sticking to the rough wool of her sweater and there were brown stains on the long, thin fingers of the hand that she held out warmly to Douglas.

Seeing his eyes drop to the dirty hand, she said, 'I'm so sorry. It's floor stain and actually it's quite dry, but I haven't had time to get it off. It'll need turps, I expect, and I can't remember where I left it. Do come in, Douglas. It's nice of you to come.'

'I didn't know you were moving in today.' Douglas stepped into the small, square hall, which was furnished with an open packing case full of books, a rolled-up carpet, a large and battered wardrobe and a copper coal scuttle that contained an electric iron, a rubber doll, a hammer and an inlaid ivory box. 'I thought it was happening tomorrow.'

"So did I,' Robina answered. 'So did Sam. That's why he's in London. And that's why there's no coal yet, and why my charwoman didn't come, and why the milk wasn't delivered, although I rang up about it last night and they said it would be, and why the floor stain isn't dry wherever I want to put anything. But still, it hasn't really gone so badly.'

'If I'd known, I'd have been glad to lend a hand—you should have rung me up,' Douglas said. 'I'm cleverer than you might think with a screwdriver.'

'Oh, you're too busy to disturb,' Robina said. 'Besides, the telephone isn't connected. It's sitting there completely dumb and unresponsive, just when I really need it. And I have had—help of a sort, shall we call it?'

She laughed and gestured at her two children, who were standing side by side in a doorway, staring at Douglas.

'Yes, we've helped a lot,' Miranda, the elder, said gravely.

Douglas never knew how to talk to children. Giving them an uneasy smile, he went on speaking to Robina. 'I don't live so very far away, after all. You could have sent for me. And I really would have been glad to help. When does Sam get back?'

'I think his train gets into Blanebury at six,' she said.

'Then it'll take him about twenty minutes to get here.' He followed her into the sitting-room, where the furniture was more or less in place, though there was no carpet on the floor and the chairs, without their loose covers, showed the varied colours of their original faded and patched upholstery. 'Martha's coming on that train,' he said.

Robina switched on an electric fire that stood in front of the empty hearth. The two children, Miranda, aged six, and Miles, aged four, came into the room and perched on the arms of chairs, keeping their steady, grave stares on Douglas.

Both children were very like Robina, thin-faced and grey-eyed, but were much fairer than she was, and about Miranda there was something intense and excitable that looked as if it could flare up easily into wild tempers or terrors. Both were dressed in grey shorts and red jerseys and were very dirty.

As Robina had not replied to what he said, Douglas repeated this time with a curious insistent note in his voice: 'Martha's coming on that train.'

'I thought she was staying in London.' Robina slumped down in an armchair and stretched out with a sigh, as if it were a great luxury to sit for a moment. 'I wonder how we're going to get that wardrobe upstairs,' she said. 'I think we'll probably have to smash it up and burn it.'

'You mean,' Douglas said, the insistent note louder, 'you thought she'd left me. That's an idea people get from time to time when she goes away. They're wrong, however. She always comes home again. And she's coming home this evening—on the same train as Sam.'

Robina gave him a thoughtful look. 'Miranda,' she said casually, 'why don't you and Miles go and take a last look at the garden before it gets too dark? And you might see if you can find another primrose in that jungle at the bottom.'

As the children ran out willingly, she went on, 'Would you believe it, they did find a primrose down there this morning—in November! Fortunately they're crazy about the garden, after six months of that furnished flat in Blanebury. It's helped to keep them out from under my feet today.'

Douglas's prominent eyes had filled with embarrassment. 'I'm sorry—of course I oughtn't to have said anything of that sort in front of them,' he said. 'I do apologize.'

'It isn't that,' she said. 'But if you want your private affairs generally broadcast and in a rather odd form, just say it all in front of them. They remember everything.'

He nodded. 'I'm not used to children, you see. By the

way, what's Sam supposed to be doing in London?'

'He's giving a paper at some scientific meeting or other,' she said. 'He and Denis Ovenden went up together. When we got the removal people's terse announcement yesterday that they were going to deliver the furniture today instead of tomorrow and that they "trusted it would be convenient" to us, he wanted to cancel going and stay at home, but obviously he couldn't do that. Anyway, I'm quite used to moving. I've really missed the charwoman more than Sam. She'd promised to come and get all the crockery washed up and cook some lunch and so on, which would have been wonderful, but of course I couldn't get her today, because she works somewhere else on Wednesdays. Actually I suppose I'm very lucky to have got her at all.' She stretched again, folding her stained hands behind her head and glancing round the half-furnished, still cheerless-looking room with a contented smile. 'It feels wonderful, you know, to be in a house of one's own at last. It certainly doesn't look much, but it's got great possibilities. You may not have noticed them yet, but my loving eye can see them.'

Douglas was watching her curiously. He had met her only a few times and he had not yet decided what she was like, or come to any conclusion as to where she fitted into the tangle of his own life. Yet it might be important to clarify this point as soon as possible. She might be a help to him, or she might be a disturbing addition to the load of distress that he already carried.

'If only I'd known . . .' he began again. But then he suddenly thought with revulsion of spending an hour or two washing up, which might easily be his fate now if he were not careful. 'If I'd known,' he went on, 'I'd at least have asked you and Sam in for dinner. As it is, I'm not sure what there is in the house. Still, if it'd be a help, I could go back and ask Miss Woods, and if there seems to be plenty of everything I could give you a ring . . . Oh, but your telephone isn't connected, is it?'

He thought he saw an amused gleam in Robina's eyes, as if she understood perfectly the thoughts that had slipped through his mind. But she answered sweetly, 'That's awfully nice of you, Douglas. I wish we could, but we've no sitter-in, and Mrs Swinson insisted on bringing us in a dinner that she's cooked at home. Sam's going to call for her on his way back from Blanebury. You know, I think we've come to live among awfully nice people.'

'I hope you'll go on thinking so,' he said heavily.

'Mrs Swinson's been an angel,' Robina said. 'She was Sam's landlady before we married—but of course you know that. That was when Sam got to know you, wasn't it? Well, she really found the house for us, at least she told us it was going to be up for sale before it had even been put in the hands of an agent, and I fell in love with it at sight, though I don't think most people understand why. Sam didn't care for it much at first, but I convinced him that we could really make something of it and at much less cost than something that we took over in better condition. And it's much more fun than taking over someone else's complete idea of a home.'

'Of course,' Douglas agreed, 'much more fun.'

In fact he could think of nothing that he would have disliked more than facing in cold blood a long campaign with builders and plumbers, and weeks spent in painting, papering and repairing, living in a smell of paint, tripping over rolls of wallpaper, searching for tools that someone else had just taken away from where he had put them down and having his mind continually prevented from slipping back into the dreams in which it found its limited measure of fulfilment.

Robina went on, 'Mrs Swinson found us Mrs Booker too. She's going to come in three times a week to clean. *Three* times—think of it! I shall sit on a cushion, and if sewing fine seams is beyond me, I can always varnish my nails. And she says she'll sit in in the evening sometimes, so that

Sam and I can get out together occasionally. She told me she lost her husband recently, so she's glad to have something to do at night. I hope to goodness the children take to her.'

'Mrs Booker?' Douglas said. 'So you've got *her* . . . But then you could come in to dinner tomorrow, couldn't you? She could stay with the children and you and Sam could come over. And Martha would be there. You—and Sam—and Martha.' He had not meant to space the words like that or to emphasize them in any special way, yet that was how they sounded to him as he spoke them.

Robina looked at him intently. 'Why did you say that like that? "So you've got *her* . . . —" as if there were something the matter with her?'

So it appeared that she had not listened to more than the first few words that he said, which was perhaps as well.

'Oh, Mrs Booker's quite all right,' he said. 'Perfectly all right. Very nice indeed, as a matter of fact. You're in luck if you've got hold of her.'

'You see, if I'm thinking of leaving the children with her,' Robina said, 'I have to be quite sure that she's all right. I liked what I saw of her and Mrs Swinson told me she'd worked for her once and how her husband was killed in an accident last winter and how everyone liked her and was so sorry for her.'

'Well, that's all quite true,' Douglas said.

'Yet you spoke in such a peculiar way, as if it meant something special.'

'I'm sorry,' he said, 'it didn't. I was only trying to ask you and Sam to dinner tomorrow evening, but . . .'

'That's *awfully* nice of you, Douglas.' A bright smile lit up Robina's thin, sharp face. 'The trouble is, I don't know yet how Mrs Booker and the children are going to get on and if those two don't take to a person they can be such utter devils. So really it would be best if we could put it off for a few days. Could we do that?'

'Of course. I just thought it might help. I just thought . . .'

He paused. He wondered whether or not to be annoyed because she had refused his invitation. The thought of what that dinner might have been like, with all its absorbing undercurrents, had an unpleasant fascination.

Robina had sat forward in her chair. Her hands were linked round her knees, over which the rough blue cloth of her jeans was tightly stretched. Her sombre, long-lashed eyes, dwelling on his, had a question in them.

'You know, Douglas, there's something about you this evening. What is it?' she asked. 'Is the book giving trouble?'

'My books never give trouble,' he answered, smiling evasively.

'I can hardly believe that,' she said.

'Well, except for the sheer grind, of course.'

'Is that what it is, sheer grind?'

'A good deal of the time.'

'But I should have thought your books sell so terrifically that you wouldn't have to grind an awful lot of the time.'

His soft mouth turned down at the corners. 'People have the most amazing misconceptions about the life of a writer,' he said. 'They think of us as favoured beings, going where we like, working when we feel like it, free as the air. In fact, the really favoured people are the ones like your husband, who get good salaries for doing exactly what they want most to do and pensions when they stop doing it. And if they're ill or worried sick, so that they can't think straight, they don't immediately find their earnings dropping and a black chasm opening up in front of them. They can even have their love affairs, when presumably they don't want to think, in relative security.'

'But you just said your books never give you trouble,' she said.

'They don't—that isn't what I meant—that isn't it at all.'

'No, I suppose it isn't,' she said.

His eyes had dropped. She was looking at his hands, and

he realized that, without his being aware of it, they had become fists. He stood up abruptly.

'I've probably been working too hard, that's all,' he said. He turned towards the door.

She got up swiftly and was out of it ahead of him. She seemed to be incapable of moving slowly. Her walk was almost a run, as if she had no time to spare for getting from one place to another.

They went out into the garden. The wind was cold but the sky was clear, with a dim, fading, bronze light along the horizon. From the garden the children's voices reached them, ringing shrilly through the dusk in the old orchard.

Douglas wanted to say something more before he left, to remove the impression that peevish speech of his must have made, but he could not think of anything to say. In his uncertainty he heard himself telling Robina, 'You know, it was down there that it happened—there at the crossroads.'

'What happened?' she asked.

'Booker's accident. A hit-and-run driver. Terrible.'

He saw her shiver. At the same time she gave him one of her odd looks.

He plunged on, 'That's murder really, when you come to think of it. Have you ever thought about murder? He was dead drunk, I believe, the poor old boy, but they say he might have been saved if he'd been taken to hospital right away, instead of left in the ditch all night. I hope you warn the children about the road. It looks quiet, but that crossroads is one of the worst spots I know. There've been several accidents there since we came to live here.'

'Thank you for telling me,' she said, 'I'll remember.'

'And if I can help in any way . . .'

'Thank you, I'll remember that too.'

'Goodbye, then.'

'Goodbye. Sam will be sorry he missed you.'

She waited by the gate, watching him as he started along the road.

He walked fast, asking himself if she could really be as simple, as unsuspicious about Sam and Martha as she sounded. For instance, could she really believe that Sam had not wanted to buy that house? It did not seem possible, for if she had nothing much in the way of looks, she seemed to have intelligence.

Yet it might be, he thought, that her intelligence was the explanation of her apparent attitude. At thirty she had been a widow, practically penniless and with two young children. Then she had succeeded in marrying a man with a safe job in the agricultural research station at Blanebury and a tolerable salary. In the circumstances, it was not unnatural for her to resolve to make the best of whatever bad job she might find she was being offered. A greater puzzle, really, than her behaviour, was what had induced Sam Mellanby to marry her.

All the same, Douglas had to admit, she had charm of a kind. Each time that he met her, he had been freshly surprised at it, having forgotten it in the interval, because he found it difficult to think about charm except as derived from beauty. Robina's charm came from her eager energy, her unselfconsciousness, her intense concentration on whatever she had on hand. It was charm, in fact, as unlike Martha's as possible.

And was that perhaps the explanation of Sam's action? People talked about acting on the rebound, and he supposed that some of them were fools enough to do it. He himself had wanted only one woman in all his life and if he lost her there would be no rebound, but only that black chasm he had spoken of, that desperate nothingness.

He walked faster still, passing the gates of his home and going on into the village towards the Lion and Lamb.

But there was no question of losing her. He had a weapon that he could always use, quite quietly, quite safely, to prevent it.

CHAPTER 2

When the six o'clock train stopped at Blanebury, Sam Mellanby and Martha Birch got off it together. They had met at Paddington and travelled down together, sitting facing one another in a crowded compartment and exchanging only a few words during the whole two hours of the journey.

Sam had read the *Spectator* and smoked a dozen cigarettes, Martha had begun by turning the pages of *Vogue*, then had let it sink into her lap and though she held it open, as if she intended to look at it again in a moment, she had turned her face towards the window and, while the autumnal twilight faded, had gazed out steadily at the passing countryside. Her grey-blue eyes with the darker rims round the irises had been wide and blank, but her mouth had been grim. Sam, who knew the meaning of most of the expressions that appeared on her face, wondered what she was up to.

Blanebury was the train's first stop and most of the people in the compartment got out there. Sitting without moving, Martha let them stumble over her feet on their way out. Sam stood up, lifted her suitcase down from the rack, stepped down onto the platform and waited. At last Martha got up and joined him, but as the crowd on the platform surged round her she stood still, looking round her as if the presence of so many people in her neighbourhood was very distasteful to her.

Sam, carrying her case and his own briefcase, said, 'Well, aren't you coming?'

He was a tall man, slender and rather angular, with straight, straw-coloured hair and thick, straw-coloured eyebrows above very light blue eyes. His face was a narrow rectangle, with a high forehead and a long, jutting chin, a

11

calm face, that gave away no more about him than was necessary. Only the lines on the forehead, which were deeper than is perhaps usual at thirty-five, suggested more nervous tension than appeared either in the set of his pleasant mouth or in his relaxed and unhurrying way of moving. He was wearing a raincoat over a dark, well-pressed and well-tailored suit that he had kept carefully for years for visits to London and for the few formal occasions that occurred in his life, such as his marriage, six months before, to Robina.

As Martha neither answered him nor moved, he said, 'I can give you a lift home, if you like, but I've got to call in at the Swinsons' on the way.'

'That,' she said bitterly, 'would be the last straw.'

'Calling in at the Swinsons'?'

'No, arriving home in your company. Douglas would probably receive you with a shotgun.'

'I shouldn't have thought you'd mind that particularly,' Sam said.

'For reasons of my own,' she said, 'of which you know nothing, I should mind very much.'

'Thank you,' he said, 'that's really nice of you. Anyway, I didn't know Douglas had a shotgun.'

'Well, then, a blunderbuss, or even a rapier or a cutlass or a claymore or any of the other unpleasant things he's got. Don't you understand?' She moved her head and looked full into his eyes. Hers had the wide, unseeing look that they had had in the train. 'Don't you understand, Sam, I'm frightened of him?'

Sam grinned. Yet her face, it was true, was paler than usual. He had noticed that in the train, but had thought that she had probably been having too many late nights in London and drinking too much. However, to succeed in being genuinely frightened of Douglas would require, Sam believed, an even more melodramatic nature than Martha's.

She was frightened of all kinds of things, of horses, of aeroplanes, of the possibility of having children, of being alone in a house, of lighting three cigarettes with one match. But she had never shown any sign of being frightened of her husband.

She said sharply, 'Don't smile like that! I'm deadly serious.'

Certainly she was serious about something. The rigidity of her features told him that, as well as the taut way that she was holding herself, which made her seem taller than usual.

She was fairly tall to start with, but because of the soft curves of her body, her slightly sloping shoulders and the smallness of her hands and feet, Sam seldom remembered it. Yet the truth was that her face, which was a short one, wide at the cheekbones and sloping into a small and delicately formed chin, was not so very far below his own. If there had been any clumsiness about her, or anything in her movements but a complete femininity, he might have thought of her as a big woman. In fact it was a thing that he noticed only when, as now, she was standing stiffly and holding her head, with the short, dark hair swept back in soft curls from her face, unnaturally high.

'Why are you going home, then?' he asked. But as he asked it the face of a man going by in the crowd caught his eye and he exclaimed, 'There's Denis! So he *didn't* miss the train . . . Just a moment, Martha, I've got to speak to him.'

Putting her suitcase down beside her, he thrust his way into the crowd and, as its movement slowed before the barrier, managed to catch up with the man and take hold of him by the arm.

'Denis, I didn't know you were on the train,' he said. 'I looked out for you at Paddington, but I didn't see you.'

Denis Ovenden looked round at him. He worked with Sam at the research station and had travelled to London with him that morning to attend the meeting at which Sam had been reading a paper on some work that they had done together. Denis was twenty-seven, heavily built, and with a square, heavy-featured but exceedingly sensitive face, and the overbright, anxious eyes of the very shy.

'I know,' he said. 'I saw whom you were with, so I stayed out of range.'

'You needn't have done that,' Sam said.

'I know. I—well, it doesn't matter at all.' He slid his arm out of Sam's grasp. 'Good night. See you tomorrow.'

'Here, wait! Don't you want a lift home? I'm stopping at your place.' For Denis occupied a room at Mrs Swinson's.

'Thanks, but I'm not going home yet, I'm going back to the lab for a bit,' Denis answered and pushed his way on through the exit.

With a worried look in his eyes, Sam turned back to where he had left Martha and her suitcase. They were not there any more.

The furrows that had brought the deep lines across Sam's forehead showed strongly for a moment. He looked round, knowing that there was no second exit from the station, but at first he could not see her, then he caught sight of her small black velvet hat in the crowd by the barrier, almost at the point where he and Denis had been standing.

With a shrug Sam started to follow her, but he made no attempt to catch up with her and was one of the last of the crowd to pass through the barrier. When he emerged, he saw her getting into a taxi. Nodding good night, he was going to pass straight on to where he had left his car that morning, when she leant out of the taxi window and called to him, 'Sam!'

He stopped beside the taxi.

'What was the trouble with Denis?' she asked.

'Just likes his own company best, most of the time,' he said. 'Unfortunately that's been growing on him ever since that affair last winter.'

'That isn't the reason,' she said. 'He doesn't like seeing you and me together.'

Sam said nothing.

She looked at him intently, then gave an irritable little shrug. 'Why *did* you do it, anyway?' she asked. 'Whatever made you do it?'

'Do what?'

'Take that house, of course. Move so near to Douglas and me. It was madness.'

'Was it?'

Her eyes blazed for a moment. 'I don't understand you, Sam. You avoided me for months, and now . . .'

'Believe it or not,' he said, 'I took that house because Robina wanted it. Besides . . .'

'What?'

'I have an idea that any objections to my living there may shortly be removed.'

Her eyes grew puzzled, then she gave a slight shake of her head. 'I don't understand you,' she repeated flatly and, withdrawing her head from the window, told the driver to start. The taxi moved on and Sam crossed the station yard to his own car.

As he started the car, the worried look that had remained on Sam's face since he had spoken to Denis Ovenden gave way to his more usual look of serenity. He had other things to think about besides Martha and Denis.

For instance, septic tanks, and the possibility of some rewiring, so that turning on two electric fires in the house at the same time did not fuse all the upstairs lights. And the question of whether or not to give in to Robina about the colour of the outdoor paintwork.

As he drove slowly through the traffic of Blanebury's main street, Sam caught himself laughing aloud. He and Robina had really quarrelled about that colour the week before, and after it had stayed sullen with each other for two days, since when they had been tactfully avoiding the subject.

Edna Swinson's house was in Blaneford, a part of Blane-bury that had been engulfed as a suburb. Threading his way through side streets, between rows of semi-detached

15

houses where there had still been fields when he first came to work in Blanebury, Sam wondered how long it would be before Burnham Priors, the village in which he and Robina had bought their house, and which was only a mile farther out of Blanebury, would suffer the same fate. When it did, he thought they would have to move, either many miles farther out or right back into Blanebury. Neither he nor Robina could endure being surrounded by trim, dreary little streets like these.

The Swinsons' house was just beyond the church in the single, wide, attractive street of the old village, a white house with two neat bay trees in tubs standing on either side of a fine old doorway. Stopping beside it, Sam pressed his thumb on his horn and kept it there until the door was opened.

'Hush now, hush!' Edna Swinson said, coming out. 'Do you want to wake the dead?'

Sam leant over to open the door of the car and she packed herself into it. She was a short, massively built, grey-haired woman in her middle fifties, who dressed strictly for comfort and economy in homemade tweed skirts and shapeless cardigans, and who wore hardly any make-up on her broad, highly coloured face, but let her imagination run riot with costume jewelry. Tonight she was wrapped up in an old raincoat and had some long, tinkling objects of pink glass dangling from her ears. She was carrying a bulky bundle, rolled up in a rug.

'It's the chicken,' she said. 'I'll have to pop the casserole in the oven for a while when we get there, but meanwhile this should keep it fairly warm . . . Iris! . . . Pete!' She put her head out of the window to shout. 'Iris, just make sure I locked the back door, will you? I think I did, but I can't quite be sure.'

'You did,' Pete Hillman said, coming out. 'I just looked.'

Edna laughed. 'That's what I like about Pete. He's made himself at home and that doesn't only mean that he's made himself comfortable, but that he's assumed responsibilities.

Would you believe it, he always remembers the day we have to put the dustbins out? He did that the second week he was here.'

Pete said, 'Hi, Sam,' and got into the car, carrying a basket which contained several bottles that clinked pleasantly against each other as he placed the basket carefully between his feet.

He had to draw his knees up almost to his chin to fold himself up in the back seat of the car, for he was very tall, with a bony, gangling kind of grace in his movements. He had dark hair cut very short, a thin parrot's beak of a nose and a sardonic mouth. He had recently come from Cornell to study in England for a year.

In his quiet, deep voice he said, 'Sherry for you and Robina, Sam—gin for Edna—scotch for me. That's the rough scheme, subject to any modification that may occur to you.'

'And what about me?' Iris asked, slamming the door of the house and jumping into the car beside him. Then she looked round in surprise. 'Where's Denis, Sam? I thought he'd be coming back with you. Isn't he coming to the party?'

'I don't think so,' Sam said. 'He went back to the lab.'

Iris exclaimed impatiently. 'Isn't he impossible? He won't get any dinner at all.'

'He can help himself from the fridge,' Edna said placidly. 'I haven't had him in the house for two years without getting the habit of leaving something there for him.'

'But he's getting worse, much worse,' Iris said. 'Don't you think so, Sam?'

He had started the car. 'I do, as a matter of fact.'

'Well, can't you do something about it?'

'What would you suggest?'

She threw herself back in her seat with a helpless gesture and might have overturned the basket that she was carrying if Pete had not saved it for her.

She was a person who made impulsive, rather violent

gestures, not because she was a particularly violent person, but rather to cover up a great deal of confused feeling. She was twenty-three, superficially a good deal like her mother, though formed from a more delicate mould.

Edna said now, 'Denis is a nice boy, but he's just a bit too intellectual for his own good. All the same, in twenty years' time we'll probably all be very proud to have known him and I'll be showing prospective lodgers that poky bedroom of his and the inkstain he made on my carpet last week and saying, "Lord Ovenden slept here." He's the only one of my lodgers I ever had that feeling about.'

'That's a kind thing to say, with Sam and me listening,' Pete said. 'But I'm glad to know your real opinion of me, Edna, after all the flattery you've served out to me these past weeks. Plain old pinhead Pete—that's all I'll ever be to you. And while we're on the subject, that inkstain isn't there any more. I took it out for you this morning.'

'You did? You darling!' she exclaimed. 'Didn't I tell you, Sam? And by the way, those drinks are Pete's contribution to the party. He insisted on taking over that side of the catering.'

Sam had been trying to express his thanks to them all ever since they had got into the car. As he did so now, however, he found that in the back of his mind there lurked the thought that to be driving home by himself to Robina and the children, to the supper of tinned soup and scrambled eggs that she could have provided in the midst of the mess, and to a quiet evening alone with her in their first real home, would have had certain great attractions.

They could have pushed two of the battered old chairs close to the fire and had their supper on their knees, then they could have sat on for a while, talking in the firelight . . .

That was as far as the thought went, for at that point he remembered that the coal had not been delivered. The room would be heated by the unsentimental warmth of an electric fire, and only one bar of it at that, because if they turned on the second bar all the lights upstairs would fuse.

But here, as it turned out, he was reckoning without Robina. When they reached the house a fire was burning in the sitting-room fireplace, a crackling wood fire that was sending long flames leaping up the chimney. Robina, changed out of her jeans and sweater into a dress of dark green wool, nylon stockings and high-heeled shoes, with her hair brushed back and pinned into a smooth coil, and with some old Spanish earrings in her ears, pointed at the fire and the pile of firewood that lay beside the hearth as that day's greatest achievement.

'Good God,' Sam said, 'you've been chopping up the wardrobe!'

'Well, it wouldn't go upstairs, and it's a horrible thing,' she said. 'I always hated it. And we're going to have built-in cupboards in the bedrooms.'

She was laughing and her eyes were brilliant. Sam put his arms round her, kissed her quickly on the forehead, then held her away from him, looking her over. In spite of her laughter and the excited welcome that she was giving her guests, he knew at once that she was desperately tired, and also that she had something on her mind. But her eyes warned him not to speak of it.

Pete was looking at the big wardrobe that filled half of the small hall. Two of its drawers were missing.

'You really have been chopping it up,' he said.

'I found some wood in the orchard too,' Robina said, 'but it wasn't dry enough for starting the fire.'

'What do you say I chop up a couple more drawers?' Pete suggested with a gleam in his eye. 'It's not often I get a chance at sheer destruction.'

Edna Swinson nudged him into the sitting-room. 'You've a job to do in there with those drinks. I must say, Robina, you've done wonders. This room's incredibly civilized already. But where are the children?'

'In bed,' Robina said thankfully. 'They said they were

19

going to stay awake and come down and take a look at you all, but really they were so tired that five minutes after I turned out the light they were out cold.'

'Well, you go and sit down now,' Edna said, 'and let Pete get you a drink, while I pop these things I've brought in the oven. By the way, have you got any ice in the fridge? Pete still can't take his whisky without it. And I suppose I'll find all the crockery I'll need in the kitchen?'

'I'll show you,' Robina said.

'No, you don't,' Edna said quickly. 'You go and sit down. I'll find everything.' She went on into the kitchen.

'I'll need some glasses,' Pete called out to her from the sitting-room, where he was unpacking his basket.

Iris said she would fetch them and followed her mother into the kitchen. For a moment Sam and Robina found themselves alone together in the little hall, beside the mutilated wardrobe.

Sam went close to her and put his hands on her shoulders. 'What is it, Robina?' he whispered into her ear.

'Douglas was here a little while ago,' she answered. 'He—' Her voice faltered. 'He tried to talk . . .'

Sam's grip on her shoulders loosened. 'Well?' he said.

She answered earnestly, 'Sam, you've got to tell me the truth about Mrs Booker.'

CHAPTER 3

Standing close to Sam in the hall, while the rattle of crockery reached them from the kitchen and the pop of a cork from the sitting-room, Robina went on, 'I *like* her, you see, Sam. But there's something about her that you've all been keeping back, and I've got to know what it is before she comes tomorrow.'

He smiled. The momentary defensive look had gone from

his face. 'All right—when the others have gone,' he said.

She accepted that and they went into the sitting-room to join Pete. A moment later Iris followed them in with a mixed lot of glasses and a bowl of ice.

'The question on my mind,' Sam said, handing cigarettes round, 'is who does the washing up after a party like this? It's your dinner but our kitchen.'

'Handled without infinite delicacy,' Pete said, 'this could become quite a social problem. Sherry, Robina?'

'For once in my life,' she answered, 'I'm looking greedily at that whisky, to put back some of the bones that seem to be missing from my spinal column.'

'Fine,' he said. 'With or without ice?'

'Oh, without.'

Iris laughed. She had squatted down on her heels on the bare floor in front of the fire.

'I've been wondering whether Pete's passion for ice in everything will survive the damp and misery of an un-centrally heated English winter,' she said.

'I believe the British drink hot tea in hot climates,' Pete said, 'so I don't see why I shouldn't drink cold whisky in cold climates. Sam?'

'Whisky, please, Pete.'

Pete sighed. 'This sherry's going to feel unwanted and it's good sherry too, the best I could get in the pub.'

'I'll have sherry,' Iris said. 'I'll leave the hard liquor to my elders and betters.'

Edna, coming in then, announced, 'The food's practically ready.'

'There's no hurry,' Sam said.

'No hurry at all,' said Robina.

'Our minds,' Pete said, 'are not really on food yet.'

In fact it was about an hour before Edna, with several drinks inside her, heaved herself onto her feet, gave a twitch to her tweed skirt, pulled down her knitted jumper and went to fetch the chicken.

For Robina it was a dreamlike hour. Sitting by the fire, sipping her drink, letting her glass be refilled, she had all at once been completely overpowered by her physical tiredness. It was not an unpleasant feeling. In fact, not to resist it, not to do anything but stretch out, warm and relaxed, in her chair, to leave most of the talking to the others while her thoughts settled into a comfortable stupor, was so agreeable that she felt as if she would not have minded if it had gone on and on indefinitely.

Drowsily she wished that she had had the time to put up some curtains to draw across the dark nakedness of the windows and that she had thought of looking in the garden for some leaves or berries to put in a vase. It would have made the room look friendlier, more welcoming to these nice people. However, there were the two primroses that the children had found, arranged carefully in a little grey and gold coffee cup and put in the middle of the mantelpiece. They at least showed good intentions.

That coffee cup ... It was one of a set that had been a wedding present at her first wedding. It was a curious feeling, seeing it again, together with all the other things that belonged to that other life. Most of the furniture here was hers. It had spent the last six months in storage and some of it, she thought, looked a little the worse for the experience. But perhaps the truth was that it was all rather shabbier than she remembered.

They had had very little money, she and Brian, and they had gone together to the cheaper salerooms and secondhand shops, optimistically promising themselves remarkable bargains and afterwards arguing themselves into a belief that some rickety piece of late Victorian furniture had at least been amazingly cheap. Of course, they had enjoyed it all.

Suddenly she felt the pricking of tears. Hurriedly putting her hands over her eyes, she rubbed them and yawned, as if it had been sheer sleepiness that made them water, and thought, looking round, that nobody had noticed anything.

Then she saw Sam looking at her. A moment afterwards he suggested that perhaps it was time to bring in the dinner.

They ate it sitting around the fire and afterwards drank coffee, which Pete went out to the kitchen to make. Their talk was mostly gossip about the research station and the neighbourhood. Many of the people mentioned were still only names to Robina, because she and Sam and the children had so far lived very much by themselves. That was what Sam had seemed to want, and Robina had not objected, though she rather hoped that now that they were in a house of their own it might be a little different. This evening, at least, seemed to promise well.

When it broke up, Sam drove the Swinsons and Pete back to Blaneford. Edna had insisted on their leaving early and the church clock in the village was striking only half past ten when he returned. He found Robina still in the same armchair, smoking a cigarette and looking more wide awake than she had earlier.

As he came to stand before the fire she gave him a quick, upward look, then lowered her eyes and, like him, gazed into the fire. It had burnt low and there was not much wood left beside the hearth. Gathering up what there was, Sam threw it into the grate.

'You want me to tell you all about Mrs Booker?' he said.

'Yes,' Robina said.

'I could have told you long ago only there was altogether too much talk going on and so—well some of us decided to shut our mouths about it. It seemed the best thing to do. But of course I could have told you. I would have if—if it had seemed important. It never occurred to me that we might actually have Mrs Booker working for us one day and that the whole thing would have to be raked up. Not that it is important, even so—to us.'

'Yet you lost your temper when I told you I'd fixed up for her to come and work here,' Robina said.

'Lost my temper? Oh—' He smiled wryly. 'You mean

about the paint. About that . . . I was meaning to tell you that I thought you were right about having the slate blue, and—'

'Sam!' she exclaimed. 'I'd decided you were right about having green.'

'So now we're in the same jam as before. What shall we do about it? Leave the final choice to Miranda and Miles?'

'For heaven's sake! They'd go into committee and tell us they'd decided on salmon pink. And until it *was* salmon pink, life would be hell. You know, the great art with those two—' She stopped herself. She did not mean to be sidetracked. 'We were talking about Mrs Booker.'

'Yes. It was all because of Denis, you see. The shutting down on the story, I mean. It had got around that it was Denis who'd killed Booker, and you can imagine—'

She interrupted. '*Denis?* Oh no!' She was deeply startled. 'It isn't possible!'

'That's what I felt about it,' Sam said. 'But the facts were these. There'd been a party at the Birches'. It was New Year's Eve. There were a good many people there and there was a lot to drink. But Denis was the only one who got drunk. Actually drunk. It was a queer business, because usually, like a good many of those extremely introverted people, he can drink a good deal without its seeming to have any effect on him. But that night he got truculent. I've an idea that there'd been some trouble before the party between him and Iris, which may have been the reason for it. At any rate, she didn't turn up and Edna had some very lame excuse for her not being there, and seemed upset about it herself. Still, that bit's guesswork on my part. The fact is, the relationship between those two changed after that evening, but I can't tell you whether that was a cause or a result of what happened.'

'So this is why you always worry so much about Denis,' Robina said. 'I've wondered a bit about that.'

'Well, it is, partly. Anyway, after making himself unpleasant all round, he left and drove off in his car. Several people tried to stop him, because he obviously wasn't fit to drive, but he got away from them and shot off along this road. Douglas and I discussed whether or not we ought to follow him, but once in the car he hadn't seemed as much out of control as he'd seemed in the house, and we didn't know what good we'd be able to do. So we went back into the house. The party broke up soon after, and none of us, driving home, noticed anything wrong at the crossroads, but next day we heard that Booker had been found dying in the ditch there, and that he mumbled something before he died about a car that didn't stop. And a couple of days after that Denis sold his car and he's never driven again since.'

'Which is just what he *would* do if . . . No!' Robina threw the stub of her cigarette into the fire. 'I don't believe it.'

Sam reached out and caught hold of her hand. 'Listen,' he said, 'that's why I never talked about it before. You say that now because you know Denis. But suppose you'd heard the story first and then met him . . . He's never got much to say for himself. He wouldn't even have tried to talk you out of the idea.'

'Denis means a good deal to you, doesn't he?' she said.

'I suppose so.'

'He brings out the protective streak in you, perhaps the same thing that made you take on me and Miles and Miranda.'

He gave her a swift, surprised look. 'No,' he said. 'Not the same thing as that at all.'

'And then he's so talented, isn't he?' she went on. 'And that appeals to you tremendously. But didn't the police do anything about it, Sam?'

'They never proved anything, one way or the other. I don't know what they really believed. Denis's story was that he'd driven straight back to the Swinsons' without mishap, put the car in the garage and gone to bed. I questioned him about it myself a few days later, after I'd heard the story going around that it was he who'd killed Booker, but he swore to me that what he'd told the police was the truth.'

'What about selling his car?'

'He told me he'd come to the conclusion that a person who couldn't trust himself to stop drinking in time, and who'd behaved as he had at the party, hadn't the right to own a car. And I know he wrote a very formal letter of apology to Douglas and Martha. It's all quite in character, to anyone who knows him at all well. All the same, in the circumstances getting rid of the car was an unlucky thing to do. I believe it's the main reason why the story's stuck as it has. And he's got more and more shut up in himself ever since, because he suspects nearly everyone of believing it, though I think he does realize that I don't and that Edna doesn't.'

'What about Iris?'

'I'm not sure about her. There's a lot about that girl that I don't understand. They still go about quite a lot together, but things seem to have got stuck at that stage. I've an idea it's being pretty bad for both of them.'

'And you were annoyed about Mrs Booker because you were afraid our having her here might make Denis distrustful of you.'

'More or less. But I shouldn't bother about that now. It would be very unfair to her to change the arrangement if she needs the job.'

'And you've nothing whatever against her?'

'Far from it.' He watched her for a moment. 'Satisfied?'

'Oh yes.'

He nodded, as if something in the way that she had answered had confirmed something in his own mind.

'Except about Douglas,' he said, 'and the other things he said when he was here.'

Robina hesitated, then said, 'I was going to tell you about

26

that. Yes, he worried me rather . . . Sam, are we going to regret having come to live here, as Iris suggested?'

'Perhaps,' he said. He let go of her hand and linked his own together, leaning closer to the fire.

'What sort of person is Douglas really?' Robina asked. 'He's always seemed to me quite nice in an indefinite sort of way, and perhaps a bit pathetic.'

'I think that's what he probably is,' Sam said.

'But I never realized how jealous of you he is. Did you? Whenever we met him, he seemed quite glad to see you. I thought he liked you. But that's why you didn't much want to come here, isn't it? I mean, his being so jealous.'

Sam did not answer. He seemed to be thinking something out, or it might have been that he was waiting for her to say something else.

She went on, speaking more unevenly, 'Personally, I don't see what difference it can make, whether we're within walking distance or only driving distance. It amounts to more or less the same thing. And you've got to live in this neighbourhood anyhow. If he doesn't like that, he could move. But he exploded about that in a queer way, saying that people think writers are free to do what they like—'

At that point Sam interrupted her, as if he had not been listening to what she had been saying. 'I travelled down with Martha this evening.'

'I know,' Robina said. 'Douglas said she was coming on that train.'

'And Denis was on that train too, but he hid in another carriage and tried to dodge us when we got out. Why d'you think that was?'

'Well, you've just said that he avoids people because he suspects them of thinking—'

He interrupted again. 'It's what I'm suspecting him of thinking that I'm talking about.' He turned towards her and took hold of her arms, gripping them hard. 'Robina, don't let anyone make trouble between us. Everything was over between Martha and me two years ago—and at that time, remember, it was I who had cause to be jealous of Douglas. But his trouble is just that he's constitutionally jealous. He doesn't need cause. And he probably half enjoys it, as one does enjoy one's obsessions, even the most miserable of them. I know I used to enjoy trying to think of a nice brutal way of killing Douglas and getting away with it. But I hadn't met you then. I didn't even know you were walking the earth.'

She stirred in his grasp and he let go of her arms but, slipping down onto the floor by her chair, slid his arms round her, pulling her close to him. She leant her cheek against his hair and with a finger tip traced the line of his thick, fair eyebrows.

'You didn't have to say all that to me,' she said. 'I knew it all, except for the murderous jealousy in your nature. I admit that's news to me.'

'Is it?' Sam said. 'Yet a little while ago, when I saw you looking round you with tears in your eyes . . . I know, I know—' as she seemed about to answer—'that's different. But I know quite as much as Douglas about jealousy.'

'Your trouble is, you know too much about what's going on inside me,' Robina said. 'If you don't get out of the habit, I'm sure you'll find yourself in for all sorts of embarrassments.'

He smiled and, lifting his face, was drawing hers down to him when her body went rigid and with a cry she jerked herself upright in the chair.

'The window! There was someone looking in at the window!'

But when Sam looked round, the dark uncurtained space of the window only reflected the lights of the room.

'There was,' Robina said. 'There was a face close to the glass.'

'All right, I'll go and see,' he said. He was getting to his feet when there was a loud knocking at the front door.

'Damn!' he said. 'You'd think we could be left alone at this time of night.'

He went out into the hall and opened the door.

Martha Birch, white-faced, dishevelled and shaking uncontrollably, was standing there. She clung to him.

'You've got to let me stay here, Sam!' she gasped. 'Douglas has just tried to kill me.'

CHAPTER 4

Robina appeared in the doorway behind Sam. Martha was trembling and her face had the blank, foolish look of shock. She had no coat on over her light dress and she was carrying no handbag.

She seemed to realize this only as she reached the fireside, for as she stood still she looked down at herself and at her empty hands and said, 'I think I'm almost out of my mind.' Then she began to cry.

Sam poured out a drink and brought it to her. She took it, gulped some of it and choked. The tears slid disregarded down her cheeks. Sam and Robina exchanged glances and Sam gave a helpless shrug. His expression puzzled Robina. It was tense and wary, with very little kindness in it. Faintly, it shocked her.

'D'you want to tell us what happened?' she asked and, putting a hand on Martha's arm, led her towards a chair.

'I told you, Douglas tried to kill me,' Martha answered. 'There's a sword on the wall over the fireplace and he—' She choked again and put a hand up over her eyes. Rather childishly she added, 'D'you know, I haven't even got a handkerchief?'

'Wait, I'll get one,' Robina said and ran out of the room.

She had only reached the bottom of the stairs when she saw that Sam had followed her out. He came close to her.

'Listen, this is all nonsense,' he whispered. 'She's putting on an act.'

'I don't think she is,' Robina said.

'I'm quite sure.'

'What would be the purpose of it?'

'That will appear presently.'

She gave him a troubled look and shook her head. 'Don't be prejudiced, Sam.'

'Well, for God's sake, don't let her stay here!'

'But if she can't go back . . .'

He swore under his breath and, turning away from her, went back into the room.

Robina ran up the stairs, searched for a clean handkerchief among suitcases that had not yet been unpacked, found one at last and went running down again.

As she came into the sitting-room she heard Sam saying, 'There isn't a bed, the sheets probably haven't been unpacked, the place is a chaos and Robina's dog-tired. If you don't want to go home, I'll drive you in to a hotel in Blanebury.'

'But I can't go like this,' Martha said. 'No coat, no luggage, no money . . . Even if they let me stay, what would they think?'

'Robina can lend you some things.'

There was such animosity in Sam's tone that Robina again felt startled and shocked. It was a tone that she had never heard from him before. It made her feel deeply uncomfortable, in a complex way that she did not at all understand.

'I can, of course,' she said, 'and it's true, as Sam said, that we haven't a spare bed, but if you'd sooner stay . . .' She hesitated because of the look on Sam's face.

Martha said quickly, 'It doesn't matter about the bed. I could lie on that sofa. And it doesn't matter about sheets. If you've just a rug or a coat or something . . . It's having people staring at me when I'm like this, seeing that I've

been crying, thinking God knows what, that I can't face.
I'm a fool about crying. I do it so easily, yet I can't bear it
when people see it.' The tears started to stream again into
the handkerchief that Robina had given her.

'Well if you're sure you'll really be all right like that . . .'
Robina said, avoiding Sam's eyes.

'*Absolutely* all right!' Martha said. 'I shan't sleep anyhow.
You're an angel, Robina. Thank you—thank you so much.
You understand what it feels like. Somehow I thought you
would.'

With a better grace than Robina had been expecting, Sam
said, 'Well, if that's settled, we may as well have drinks all
round, then you can tell us the rest of it. But I may as well
tell you, Martha, I haven't believed a word you've told us,
so far.'

Looking up at Robina, Martha managed to produce a
dim, watery smile. 'He never believes anything you tell him,
does he?'

'It's his scientific training,' Robina said, responding to
the smile.

'Oh, I don't think it is,' Martha said. 'I think it's just
that he's an awful liar himself. Liars always distrust other
people.'

Sam had gone to the table where Pete's bottles stood and
was holding them up, one after the other, to see what was
left in them.

'I wish we'd had sherry earlier and kept the whisky for
this crisis,' he said, 'but Martha's just had the last of it.' He
poured out two glasses of sherry.

'It looks as if you've been having a party,' Martha said.

'Just the Swinsons and Pete,' Sam said. 'Now go on,
Martha.' She leant back in her chair and closed her eyes.
After a moment she said quietly, 'There's something you
may as well know. I'm in love and I want Douglas to divorce
me.'

Robina saw Sam's head jerk up. Then he looked down

again at his glass, drank some sherry and said, 'Well, well.'

Martha ignored him. She kept her eyes, the gaze of which was now quite steady, on Robina.

'While I've been in London, he—this man—has been coming to see me,' she said. 'Douglas knows nothing about it. When I told him this evening that I wanted him to divorce me, I didn't tell him the real reason. He's such a morbid, violent person, under that quiet manner of his— perhaps you don't believe that, but it's the truth, I found it out long ago—I didn't know what he might do. So I told him simply that I didn't think we'd ever be happy together and that we ought to break it up. We could call it mental cruelty. He could say I was always throwing teacups at him, or something. I believe you can get a divorce for that nowadays.'

'You were tact and gentleness itself,' Sam murmured.

She swung round on him. 'Do stop the sarcasm, Sam! I'm trying hard to keep my head and tell this simply.' The shake was back in her voice.

'I'm sorry,' Sam said. 'Go on, Martha.'

'I dare say I was a fool, the way I went about it,' she said. 'It might have been better to tell him the truth. Or perhaps I should just have realized that it was hopeless. It was, of course. He hardly listened to me. Instead, he started to tell me that I'd got to go to America with him, that if I wouldn't he wasn't going to let me have any more money. He seemed to think that threat would settle everything, as if he'd forgotten that I was earning my own living until I married him and that I mightn't necessarily be afraid of doing it again. I told him that. I told him that in fact I'd far sooner keep myself than trail around the world with him. And that—that was when he reached for that horrible sword!'

'America,' Sam said. 'I didn't know he was thinking of going there.'

'Next month,' she said, 'when this book's finished. And

he wants to stay for about six months, if he can get the dollars.'

'You know,' Sam said, 'that almost sounds as if he's more suspicious than you think.'

She shook her head sharply. 'That's coincidence. He's been talking for ages of going there.'

'Well, what are you going to do about it?'

'That's what I don't know yet. I've just been thinking . . .'

'Well?'

She looked down at her hands, folded in her lap, and spoke hesitantly. 'I've been thinking that if you would go and talk to him, tell him that I really mean what I said to him—'

'*Me?*' Sam exclaimed with a start. 'You want *me* to do that?'

'Yes,' Martha said. 'He's got a great regard for you. He takes you seriously.'

'No!' Sam said violently. 'Once and for all—no!'

'Oh, please!' she said pleadingly. 'Robina, what do you think? Don't you think that Douglas might listen to Sam?'

To Robina, remembering her talk with Douglas that afternoon, it seemed certain that any interference by Sam would do more harm than good to Martha.

She answered evasively, 'You both know Douglas better than I do. But I'd be sorry if Sam came home with that sword sticking into him.'

'Just my feelings, in all their naked simplicity,' Sam said.

'Oh, Sam dear, don't be so silly,' Martha said. 'It's because Douglas would *listen* to you that I'd like you to go to him. And besides, I think you ought to help me, because you know that you and Robina would much prefer it if I weren't around here any more. That's only natural, however well we all behave about it, and in your place I'd feel the same. And actually, you almost told me so at the station, didn't you? You said you thought that any objections to your living here might shortly be removed. Isn't that what you meant—that you thought my marriage wasn't going to stand up much longer?'

Sam showed embarrassment. 'Even so, I'm not going to do it, Martha. And to check further unpractical suggestions, I propose that we all try to get some sleep now and talk about it again in the morning. If I can think of anything that might be helpful I'll tell you, but please put that particular idea right out of your mind.'

Martha gave a sigh. 'All right, we'll talk about it in the morning. And thank you both for being so good to me.'

But in the morning, Robina thought, as she went to fetch blankets and a pillow and a nightdress for Martha, Sam would find that Martha had not put that idea out of her mind. The same proposal, perhaps with some new twist and a few embellishments, would be put to him again, and with a persistence and a deafness to argument that in the end might drive him, through sheer exasperation, to do what Martha wanted.

For that was the kind of person that Martha was, and that was the kind of person that Sam was too.

The thought worried Robina. She had been ready to shelter Martha and had been troubled by Sam's uncharacteristic hostility to her, but she felt a forceful and uncomplicated dislike of the idea of his becoming involved in Martha's problems.

Going to bed presently in a cold and unswept bedroom, without curtains at the windows or rugs on the floor, she said, 'I saw in Martha's eye that she'll come back to that idea tomorrow, Sam. But apart from anything else, tomorrow I'm putting you to work here. There are hundreds of things for you to do.'

Sam grinned. 'So you're regretting your hospitable impulse already, are you? I thought you might.'

'No,' Robina said, 'but I'm ready to start regretting it tomorrow if she gets under our feet with her difficulties.'

'Don't worry,' he said. 'If she doesn't want to go home I'll get her into a hotel somehow, or possibly Edna could let her have a room.'

Robina yawned. Sitting down on the edge of the bed, she kicked off her slippers. 'This floor's all splinters,' she said. 'We'll have to do something about it.' She felt as if, the moment she lay down, she would fall fast asleep. 'But you do seem to hate her rather immoderately, Sam. Isn't it time you grew out of it?'

He did not reply at once. Then he muttered, 'I thought I had.'

'She must have hurt you very badly once if you still feel it like that.'

To this Sam made no reply at all, or if he did, it took so long to come that Robina had fallen into a deep sleep before he had said anything.

CHAPTER 5

In the morning Robina was awakened by whispering, conspiratorial voices on the landing. Pushing herself up onto an elbow, she saw the doorknob turn. Then it turned back again without the door having opened. A moment later this was repeated.

A voice outside said, 'Silly, I'll do it.'

There was a clink of china, then the door was thrown wide open. Robina saw Miranda, in her pyjamas, bending down to pick up a cup and saucer from the floor, where she must just have set them down. Gripping the edges of the saucer with both hands and holding it out well in front of her, she advanced step by step into the room, her gaze riveted on the slopping tea.

Miles, looking ashamed of his defeat by the door, followed close behind her.

35

'The lady made it,' Miranda explained as she delivered the tea safely to Robina.

'Don't I get some too?' Sam asked.

'I'm going to fetch it now,' Miranda said. 'I have to carry them one at a time, you see. Miles is so silly, he'd drop it.' She ran out.

Miles climbed up on the foot of the bed. 'Why is the lady there?' he asked.

'She came on a visit,' Robina said.

'Why?'

'I suppose she likes us. That's the usual reason.'

'How come?'

'She has a good heart, she likes everybody' Sam said.

Miles digested this unconvincing piece of information sitting back on his heels and frowning. With a strange feeling about her heart, Robina saw suddenly that in a little while, when he had had time to pick up a few more of Sam's mannerisms, everyone would take him, with his fair colouring and rather long face, for Sam's child.

'What's the lady doing now?' she asked.

'She's having tea too.'

'Well, she has her points as a visitor,' Robina said, 'but we'd better get up, I suppose, and take over.'

She put her empty teacup down on the floor, swung her feet out of the bed and stood up.

When she went downstairs, dressed again in her jeans and sweater, she found Martha looking unexpectedly fresh after her night on the sofa, with normal colour in her cheeks, while her grey-blue eyes, with the dark rims round the irises, were bright and cheerful. Either she had thought of a way out of her troubles or had decided not to worry about them any more.

They got the breakfast together, Martha organizing the children into a belief that they were helping too with a skill that surprised Robina. The children took to her and in a gay and casual way she was very charming with them.

While they were all at breakfast Mrs Booker arrived.

She came to the back door, dressed in a worn brown coat, with a coloured scarf tied over her head. She carried a cretonne bag that turned out to contain a print apron and some down-at-heel black slippers. She was a short, sturdily built old woman with a warm smile and candid, intelligent brown eyes.

Taking in the situation in the kitchen, she said to Robina, who had let her in, 'Well, you did get on well yesterday, Mrs Mellows. I was very sorry I couldn't help the first day, like I thought I could, but Wednesdays I always go to Miss Harber down at Greenacres. I've been going there for thirteen years, so I wouldn't want to disappoint her. Now what would you like me to get on with?'

Robina was to discover that, reliable as Mrs Booker might be in all other respects, she was never to be trusted about names. The Miss Harber she had just mentioned turned out to be in fact a Miss Harbottle, and the name of Mellanby, in spite of all attempts at correction, settled into Mellows. Two syllables, Mrs Booker seemed to feel, should be enough for anyone.

Robina suggested that she should get on with the washing up that she herself had not been able to tackle the day before. There were cooking pots and piles of plates with the dust and straw from the packing cases in which they had arrived still sticking to them. Putting on her print apron, Mrs Booker took off her well-polished brown shoes, put on the slippers she had brought, pushed up the sleeves of her grey knitted cardigan and got to work.

Robina went back to the sitting-room and poured out another cup of coffee.

'It's going to be all right,' she said delightedly, 'I'm sure it is.'

She had made up her mind to get started at once on her own work without asking Martha what she intended to do. Drinking the coffee quickly, she went running upstairs, made the bed in her room and Sam's, then began a campaign of scrubbing out cupboards and drawers, so that later in the day she could unpack their clothes and put them away. She had slept off all her tiredness and enjoyed the work, which she went at in her usual thorough but hasty way, slopping water over her jeans and thoughtlessly sweeping back her hair from her face with a wet hand.

Presently Sam, who had dressed that morning in his oldest clothes, put his head in at the door.

'Okay if I start unpacking the books?' he asked.

Robina sat back on her heels. 'Yes, but those bookcases ought to be polished up a bit first.'

'Where do I find the polish and things?'

'I think they're in the cupboard under the stairs, in an old biscuit box.'

Sam withdrew his head and she heard him go downstairs and soon afterwards, from the clear, carrying voices of the children, she was able to deduce that he was unpacking the books under their instructions.

Presently Robina finished work in the bedroom and, leaving drawers and cupboard doors open, went to the window to open it to its fullest extent, to help dry out the freshly scrubbed wood. She saw Martha in the orchard, and Sam with her. They were walking up and down, smoking and talking earnestly.

For a moment Robina stayed motionless at the window. Then she swung away from it.

There was no need for her to pretend to herself that she was anything but intensely jealous of every moment of intimacy that Sam had enjoyed with Martha. But the important thing, she thought, was not to let the little flame of unreasoning hatred that this jealousy had kindled in her heart gain such a hold on her emotions that it burnt up all her kindlier feelings for Martha. On the whole too, she thought, it was probably important not to give the feeling away to Sam any more than she could help.

Deciding to go downstairs and make some tea for Mrs Booker, she had started down when Miranda came rushing up to meet her.

'A man came to the door,' she said excitedly.

'The coal!' Robina exclaimed hopefully.

'No, it isn't,' Miranda said. 'His face is clean; besides, he's got some brussels sprouts and his name is Ringrose. He says he's a neighbour, so I took him in the sitting-room. Miles is looking after him.'

The name Ringrose conveyed nothing to Robina. Commending Miranda on her social tact, she went to the sitting-room and found Miles and a man there, both silent and each keeping what seemed a rather wary eye on the other.

The stranger was a short, narrow-shouldered yet wiry-looking man of about forty, with a thin face marked by harsh lines from his nostrils to the corners of his mouth and a deep cleft in his chin. His skin and his lank, badly cut hair were almost the same shade of drab and his small, sharp eyes were a greenish brown. He was wearing threadbare tweeds and gum boots and was holding a large basket full of brussels sprouts.

As Robina greeted him he smiled and gestured apologetically at his boots. The smile was tight-lipped and uneasy.

'I'm sorry about these, Mrs Mellanby,' he said. 'I never meant to come in with them, but the little girl wouldn't let me off. I just wanted to introduce myself and say I live in the red bungalow opposite and if there's anything Mrs Ringrose or I can do to help while you're moving in, we'll be only too glad. If there's anything you'd like to borrow, I mean, before your own things are unpacked, and so on. And I brought you over these sprouts, because I know there's nothing in the garden here and vegetables are the one thing it's hard to get in the country till you've got some of your own going.'

'That's very good of you, Mr Ringrose!' Robina said

warmly. 'It's quite true, there isn't a thing in the garden except the fruit trees.'

'And you won't get anything off them unless you prune them hard,' he said. 'And if you do that you still won't get the fruit, because the village kids'll get them all. They'll swarm all over the place the moment your back's turned. And there's nothing you can do about it. If you catch one and take a stick to him, his father'll have you up for assault. My advice to you is cut 'em all down and make a nice lawn there, then you'll be rid of the nuisance and be just as well off in the end.' The little twitching smile stayed there all the time he was talking.

Robina said, 'That sounds a little drastic.'

'Well, you wait and see what it's like,' he said. 'They're not nice people hereabouts, you can't trust them an inch. They all expect to get something for nothing and none of them know the meaning of real work. They're a very ignorant class of people and the government's making them worse, pampering them and their kids till they don't expect to have to raise a finger to look after themselves. Of course you could put up barbed wire all round, but I don't say that'll work. They've got ingenuity, I'll say that for them.'

'I don't think I should like it much either,' Robina said.

'Then just cut all the trees down, that'll settle 'em. They won't pinch what they can't eat.' He smiled so steadily that Robina wondered if she had been intended to take all that he was saying as a joke. 'Meanwhile if you'd like any vegetables any time, I can always fix you up. I've got a small market garden nothing much, and I sell most of my stuff in Blanebury, but I can always oblige a neighbour. Now I won't keep you any longer when I know you've a lot to do. Pleased to have met you.'

Robina repeated her thanks. She began to wonder, however, whether the brussels sprouts were in fact a present, as she had at first thought them, or whether she ought to offer to pay for them. But he left promptly, without any signs of

40

expecting payment, and refusing even to wait until she could empty the basket and return it to him.

'No hurry about it,' he said. 'Any time that's convenient.'

When he had gone Robina took the basket out to the kitchen.

'Look what Mr Ringrose brought me,' she said.

Mrs Booker, who was just washing out the tea cloths she had been using, gave them a sudden fierce twist as she wrung them out.

'Well, isn't that nice of him?' she said in a tone of obvious insincerity.

'I'd wondered who lived in that bungalow,' Robina said.

'He's lived there five years,' Mrs Booker said.

'Well, these are wonderful sprouts. Mr Ringrose must be a good gardener.'

'He seems to do all right, he's got television and everything. Still, they don't waste their money, those two. Sometimes I'm sorry for Mrs Ringles, she never goes anywhere. And he don't smoke and you never see him having a pint in the Lion. That's sense, these days. Reckon I couldn't be very keen meself, though, on a man who never had any fun. My old man—' She stopped. She shook out the cloths that she had washed. 'Where shall I put these to dry?' she asked.

'Just anywhere,' Robina said. 'I haven't fixed anything up yet. I think I'll make some tea now.'

'That'd be nice,' Mrs Booker said. 'I can always drink tea any time.' She hung the tea cloths from the edge of the draining board. Turning again to the sink and swishing some water around in it, she went on, 'Maybe you've heard about my old man, Mrs Mellows. I mean about him being drunk when he had his accident. I dare say it's true, but I wouldn't like you to think he was ever a drinker, I mean, what you'd call a *drinker*. And when he'd had a glass or so too many, he always knew how to behave himself. You could always count on that. He'd never behave rough or use bad language. Really, the more he'd had, the politer he got.

He'd go to the door and hold it open for you and call you madam. Sometimes it made me laugh fit to bust.' She turned to look at Robina with a smile on her lips. 'I often had a good laugh at the little fellow,' she said. 'He never minded. We were married nearly forty years and if I'd gone to that New Year's party with him at his sister's he'd be alive now, but I wasn't feeling too grand that night, so I stopped at home. But I said to him, "You go on without me," I said, thinking he'd enjoy himself, what with his nephew being home from Kenya and all . . . It's me knees, you know.' She sat down on a kitchen chair and started rubbing them. 'Sometimes they get bad in the cold weather, like it was then. Usually I do all right if I just take a pinch of mustard every day in a cup of coffee with my supper, but when they get extra bad I take two aspirins and lay down and a small glass of rum when I go to sleep. But a pinch of mustard every day in a cup of coffee is the best thing there is.'

As Robina made the tea Mrs Booker went on chattering comfortably about her infirmities and her various means of tackling them.

They were in the midst of a discussion of the troubles that afflict the kidneys, sitting facing one another at the kitchen table and drinking tea, when Robina heard Sam come into the house. Going to look for him, she found him in the room where the books were, a small room that they had decided should be his study, but he was not attending to the books, which were in heaps all over the floor. He was sitting on the arm of a chair, smoking a cigarette and gazing blankly at the empty bookcases.

As Robina came in, he looked round at her. 'Well, I said I would talk to Douglas,' he said.

'I thought you had,' she said.

'I'm a fool.'

She gave a wry smile. 'The girl has a way with her.'

'That's the truth. But I'm a fool all the same. It won't do any good.'

'Will it necessarily do any harm?'

'It might, don't you think?'

'But you don't really think so.'

'Not really. All the same . . .' He reached out for her, put an arm round her and pulled her into the chair beside him. 'I can't make up my mind what she's up to, and I may as well tell you, I've discovered that I'm mortally afraid of her.'

Robina felt a sudden unevenness in the beating of her heart 'Then it *is* a good thing we came here,' she said. 'It'll be kill or cure.'

'I hope it doesn't actually have to come to killing . . . For God's sake!' For someone had just rang the front doorbell. 'I thought one had peace and quiet in the country!'

'The coal!' Robina said, and was scrambling out of the chair to run to the front door when she heard the firm tread of Mrs Booker, passing the door.

By the time Robina reached the hall Mrs Booker had opened the front door, but because she had opened it only a little way and looked out cautiously, as if ready to defend the house from the entry of some undesirable person, Robina could not see who was there. It seemed to her, however, that the silence while Mrs Booker and the visitor regarded one another lasted unusually long.

Then she heard Mrs Booker say quietly, 'Good morning, Mr Oving.'

Robina knew her well enough by now to be able to tell that the visitor was Denis Ovenden.

CHAPTER 6

The thought of the effort that it had cost Mrs Booker to hide her feelings, to speak with courtesy, to act with such propriety, moved Robina deeply. For she had no doubt, as

Mrs Booker let Denis in and tramped back to the kitchen, showing Robina as she passed a face that looked ten years older than it had a few minutes before, that the old woman believed that it was Denis who had killed her husband and left him to die in the ditch. That there was no hatred in her eyes, but only a muddled and sad sort of pity, made her lined, dejected face only the more tragic.

Denis's heavy face had flushed at sight of her and he stood there, looking as if he were about to go blindly out of the house.

Wishing that Sam had warned her sooner, so that something so painful to the two people concerned need never have happened, Robina's thoughts took a selfish turn and she wondered, 'Which do we lose now, a friend or our domestic help?'

Luckily Miranda and Miles adored Denis. Each taking possession of a hand, they led him into the sitting-room and a conducted tour of the house and garden.

Like many very shy people, incapable of making advances to children, Denis was surprised but always delighted when they took to him and was ready to give an amount of thoughtful attention to their conversation to which they were not at all accustomed. After a while he would be exhausted by them and need rescuing, but particularly at such a moment as this, Robina thought, their love was the perfect antidote to the effects of his meeting with Mrs Booker.

Domestic sounds had started again in the kitchen, so at least Mrs Booker had not felt that she must walk straight out of the house because of her meeting with Denis. In fact she did not leave until about twenty minutes after the time at which she was supposed to leave. On her way out she came to see Robina again.

'I was thinking,' she said as she tied her scarf over her head, 'if you'd like it, Mrs Mellows, I could ask Mr Darley about some wood. You can't tell these days when they'll bring the coal, but I know Mr Darley's got some logs and they'd help out till you get the coal. It isn't nice to be without anything to burn in your fireplace this time of year. The electric's very handy, but it isn't the same, so if you like I'll go and speak to Mr Darley. I seen him sawing it up in his yard, so I know he's got it.'

Robina answered that the more logs Mr Darley could bring the better.

'All right then,' Mrs Booker said. 'I'll go and speak to him on my way home.'

When she had gone Robina went to work in the kitchen with a tin opener, preparing lunch. Both Martha and Denis, she thought resignedly, as she laid places on the kitchen table, would probably stay. A pity, since so far as she knew they did not like one another. When the meal was ready she went to the kitchen door and shouted for everyone to come. Only Martha appeared. Robina shouted again. This brought the children, holding out grubby hands and protesting that they were far too clean to need washing. A third shout still failed to bring Sam and Denis. She went looking for them.

They were in Sam's room, talking.

'Nothing doing,' Denis was saying as Robina came in. 'The phenylalanine seems to have no effect on the damn thing at all.'

'That's curious, isn't it?' Sam said. 'One might expect it to do something since you found tyrosine quite active.'

'Yes, it was active, but only immediately after application—' Denis, becoming aware of Robina, stopped, looking vaguely embarrassed, as if he were not sure where he had met her before.

Robina said to Sam, 'Didn't you hear me?'

'Oh yes,' he said, 'yes, of course. We were just coming.'

'But look here, I'm not staying,' Denis said. 'I only looked in to see if I could lend a hand somehow. I didn't mean to thrust myself on you for lunch.'

'Of course you're staying,' Sam said.

'It's all out of tins anyway,' Robina said. 'Come along.'

Denis tried to argue, but Sam took him by the arm and thrust him towards the door. In the kitchen the children fortunately took charge of him again. They had so much to ask and so much to tell that his continuing embarrassment as well as Martha's silent brooding on her troubles could be ignored. Then when lunch was over Martha volunteered to do the washing up and Denis, as if determined to do something to justify his presence, said that he would help her. Robina flew upstairs and began unpacking clothes and putting them away in the clean drawers and cupboards.

She did not know when Sam and Denis left the house. Sam did not come to tell her that they were leaving, but vaguely afterwards she remembered having heard the car start.

Martha had established herself in the sitting-room with some old curtains that Robina had handed over to her and was cutting and stitching them to fit the sitting-room windows. While she did this she told the children stories. This was something at which Robina had no skill. She could read aloud with a good deal of dramatic verve, but she lacked inventiveness. Coming and going in the house, overhearing snatches of Martha's stories and catching glimpses of the children's absorbed faces, Robina decided that this was not a lack from which Martha suffered.

But presently Martha went too far. Robina would have recognized the danger signs: the rigidity of Miranda's body, the quickening of her breath, the glazed look of her eyes. If Martha noticed these things she mistook them for tributes to her storytelling, and she went on, quite absorbed in it herself, until with a wild wail Miranda leapt to her feet and rushed from the room.

She went on screaming until she found Robina, clutched her tightly and hid her face against her.

'She says our wardrobe belongs to a three-footed witch!"

she shrieked. 'She says she started living in it when it was in the store place but she'll find it and come and live in it here and be angry because the drawers are lost. Mummy, I don't like three-footed witches—I don't *like* them!'

Robina put her arms round her. As Martha and Miles came hurrying after her, Martha looking shocked with remorse and Miles coolly interested, Robina crooned gently to the trembling child, then began to explain that, in the first place, the witch was only in a story and didn't really exist; in the second place, was a very kind witch, who had only been looking after the furniture, at Robina's request, while it was in store; in the third place, never spent the winter in Britain, because it wasn't cold enough for her, and was by now in Siberia.

This form of reassurance had been likened by Sam to the defence in a libel case. 'In the first place, the words complained of were not spoken, and in the second place, they were justified . . .' There was, at all events, much the same sort of attempt to cover all possibilities.

Martha, looking shaken herself, said, 'I can't tell you how sorry I am, Robina. I thought I was being so clever and got carried away. I don't know how I could be such a fool. It's such a horrible thing being frightened.'

She spoke the last sentence with such a strength of feeling that Robina, who had been intensely irritated at her stupidity, felt more forgiving.

'Miranda's imagination gives us all a bit of trouble,' she said. 'We're hoping that, living here and being settled, she may start to grow out of it.'

'My imagination gives me a good deal of trouble still,' Martha said. 'I've never grown out of it, so I ought to have known. Sometimes I think it would help if I could write or something but the most I can do is give Douglas ideas when he gets stuck. I can always think of something fantastic to get him out of a difficulty . . . What is it, Miles?' For he was tugging at her skirt.

'What does she use her third foot for?' he asked.

Martha laughed, picked him up and carried him back to the sitting-room, where she satisfied his curiosity safely out of earshot of Miranda.

Robina kept Miranda with her for a while, chatting to her and giving her small jobs to do while she herself went on with her work. As the time passed she began to wonder why Sam had not come home, thinking that his mission to Douglas was occupying a rather longer time than she considered necessary. But possibly he had driven on into Blanebury, to look in at the laboratory for a little while. To keep him away from it for a whole day was always exceedingly difficult.

This thought did not quite dispel the discomfort she felt as her imagination, not perhaps as vivid as Martha's, but at times active enough, told her of all the different things that might have happened during Sam's interview with Douglas. If Douglas had really behaved as Martha had told them, and if he believed, as Robina thought he had been trying to hint to her the day before, that Martha and Sam were lovers, then something very unpleasant might have taken place.

A beautiful way, she thought viciously, to start off their life in Burnham Priors, the life that was to be so settled and secure and good for the children, whose lives so far had been far from settled and secure!

But what reason could Douglas possibly have for his suspicions of Sam? Surely even the most morbidly jealous person needed some tiny grain of evidence before the horrible weed could really start to sprout in his mind. Or was that not so? Could it all grow out of the past, watered perhaps by a few idle rumours? But if there were rumours, who was spreading them?

These questions made Robina so restless that, although she was as tired when she had given the children their tea and put them to bed as she had been at the same time the day before, she could not face the idea of sitting down in the same room as Martha, talking to her about heaven knew what, even Sam perhaps, and making the effort that her self-respect would demand to conceal that she had anything on her mind.

Putting on the coat that was hanging on a peg in the hall, she went to the kitchen and emptied Mr Ringrose's brussels sprouts into a basin. With his basket on her arm, she looked into the sitting-room.

'I'm just going over to the Ringroses' to return this basket,' she said. 'I think they're both asleep upstairs, but you don't mind listening, just in case of trouble, do you?'

During the afternoon Martha had transformed the sitting-room. She had hung up the curtains, put the covers on the chairs and a rug in front of the fireplace. Since Robina had last looked into it, the room had become a cheerful and charming place.

As warmly as she could she added, 'You've really done wonders in here. Thank you ever so much.'

'It's been a great help to me,' Martha said. 'I'm never going to be able to thank you enough. Why d'you think Sam's so long?'

A discussion of that was just what Robina wanted to avoid. 'I expect he went in to the lab for a bit,' she said. 'So far as I can make out, there are always switches needing turning on or off, or something like that, and sometimes I think he just needs to reassure himself that the place hasn't burnt down while he looked the other way.'

'All the same, I wish he'd come back,' Martha said sombrely.

'Well, I'll be back in a few minutes,' Robina said.

'Not if Mrs Ringrose has anything to do with it,' Martha answered. 'Once she starts talking, you'll never get away.'

In fact Robina was gone for about an hour. The Ringroses' bungalow was set far back from the road, half concealed from it by a row of cypresses. It was small, square and built of red brick, and, because it was surrounded by bare earth and rows of vegetables, without any lawn or flowering plants to be seen, gave Robina, approaching it in the dusk, a curious impression of desolation.

She found Mrs Ringrose alone. She was a woman of about her own age, pretty in a soft, plump way, but already with varicose veins and a sagging look about what might have been a good figure. She was wearing a print overall, no stockings and quilted bedroom slippers trimmed with swansdown. Her fair hair hung loose on her shoulders.

When she came to the door to answer Robina's ring she was wearing spectacles, but as soon as she saw that it was a visitor and not a hawker or tramp at her door she took them off. Without them, such intelligence as there had been in her face disappeared. Her eyes were large and blue, and as their muzzy, unfocused gaze fastened on Robina they looked mournfully puzzled but eager to please.

'You're Mrs Mellanby, aren't you?' she said. 'You'll have to excuse me—the way I'm dressed, I mean. I wasn't expecting anyone. I don't see many people. So I get careless and I've just been making a pie—just popped it in the oven —well, you know how it happens. I meant to get dressed properly ages ago . . .'

She paused as she saw Robina's jeans below the hem of her coat, gave a vague smile as if the sight reassured her and invited Robina to come in.

Robina tried to return the basket and leave immediately, but the invitation became pressing. She went in and found a small sitting-room, as spotlessly clean and well kept as Mrs Ringrose was sloppy, with a bright fire in the tiled fireplace, flowering plants on the window sill, crisply ironed, embroidered antimacassars on the backs of the chairs, and dominating the room, as Mrs Booker had said, a fine television set.

Mrs Ringrose saw Robina glance at this and smiled proudly. 'Mr Ringrose bought me that a month ago for my birthday,' she said. 'It makes all the difference. Really, that's what I was doing when you came. Like I said, I'd just popped the pie in the oven and I was sitting down to look for a little while. Have you got television?'

'No,' Robina said.

'Oh well, you'll get it soon,' Mrs Ringrose said comfortingly. 'You wouldn't believe the difference it makes. Of course, that's what one says every time, isn't it? First, when we bought the car, I thought, "I don't need anything else, this is all I want to be really satisfied." Then one day Harold comes home with the washing machine and soon I can't think how I ever got on without it. Have you got a washing machine?'

'Yes,' Robina said.

'They're wonderful, aren't they?'

Mrs Ringrose had sat down and folded her hands in her lap. They were big and strong and far better tended than the rest of her.

'Of course, it means you do a lot more washing really, not sending things to the laundry,' she said, 'and then there's the ironing. I've got a steam iron, which makes all the difference, but still, it's a lot of work. I expect you've got a refrigerator. I wish I had one, but that's what we're going to get next. I should think you find it a great help. It saves on the shopping and all, doesn't it?'

'Yes, it makes all the difference,' Robina heard herself say. 'But really, I mustn't keep you. I only came to return the basket and thank you so much for sending the sprouts.'

'Only too glad,' Mrs Ringrose said. 'But you won't go yet, will you? You'll stay for a cup of tea?' The voice was eager and the muzzy, vague eyes suddenly betrayed anxiety.

Robina began to say that she really could not stay, but Mrs Ringrose, in a voice that had become almost imploring, assured her that she had been just about to make some tea for herself. Robina was sure that this was not true, but saw that the other woman was so lonely that she could not bear the thought of losing so quickly the only visitor that she had perhaps had for weeks.

Staying on, Robina had tea with Mrs Ringrose and listened to all her plans for improving the bungalow.

'Sooner or later,' she said presently, dropping her voice as if she were bringing an awesome subject into the conversation, 'we're going to put in central heating! It's expensive, of course, but all the time it's putting up the value of the property, and then if we sell . . . Well, I'd like to sell and move away sometime, I think. I'm not really all that fond of living in the country myself, but Harold got ill at the works in Islington and the doctor told him he'd got to go and live in the country. He seems well enough now though, and sometime perhaps . . . But Harold says he won't move till he's shown the people here a thing or two. You know how it is with people in a place like this, they don't believe you belong to the human race till you've lived among them twenty years.'

She would have gone on indefinitely and Robina would have found it very hard to get away if Harold Ringrose had not come in.

He made it only too easy for her to leave. He was plainly very put out at finding her there. He made no attempt to wear the forced smile that he had kept on his thin, drab face throughout his morning visit, and seemed almost suspicious of her motives in coming to see his wife.

It seemed to Robina that he was in a state of excitement, perhaps anxious to pour out to his wife the story of some injury that he had just received, and that he found the presence of a stranger in his home an almost unbearable frustration.

Blundering her way back through the darkness along the path to the road, for neither of the Ringroses had offered to guide her along it, Robina found herself thinking what ill luck it was for her and Sam that this couple should be their nearest neighbours.

She has just reached home and was fumbling in her bag for her latchkey when a car drew up at the gate and Sam and Pete got out of it. Sam was telling Pete that he had always been extremely puzzled by the apparent metabolic inertness of the nucleus and Pete was saying that it certainly was puzzling. From the fact that they were both talking at the same time and with rather more animation than seemed called for, Robina deduced that the earlier part of the conversation had taken place in the Lion and Lamb. They did not see her until she opened the door, the light from inside showing her to them, outlined on the doorstep.

'Where've you been to?' Sam called out, pushing open the gate and crossing the little courtyard.

'It'd be more to the point to tell me where you've been, except that I can guess,' she answered. In a low voice she added, 'How did it go with Douglas?'

He replied in her ear, 'I'll tell you about it later.' His tone was cheerful, as if the interview had left no scars.

Pete had followed him in. 'That's a nice pub,' he said. 'Nice and friendly, nice atmosphere, nice earthy talk going on. I'm going to see a lot of the inside of that pub, Sam, now that you and Robina have come to live so close.'

'It seemed to me that you weren't quite a stranger there,' Sam said as they went indoors. 'Seemed to me the landlord knew your face already.'

'Well, I've been using up my spare time investigating the British way of life—and believe me, there's a lot of it around here—' Pete stopped, because he had nearly trodden on a folded piece of paper that was lying on the doormat. 'This anything important?' he asked, holding it out to Robina.

She smoothed it out and looked at it under the hall light.

'The logs!' she cried. 'It's a note from Mrs Booker's friend Mr Darley. She said she was going to ask him if he could let us have some logs, to tide us over till the coal comes. He must have delivered them while I was at the Ringroses'. Now we'll really have a fire. Martha—'

She was just going to call out to ask about the delivery of the logs when Martha appeared at the door of the sitting-room, and something about the look on her face, though for a moment Robina did not know what it was, stopped her in the middle of the question.

Then she realized that Martha's appearance had had the same effect on Pete and Sam, though in Pete it was intensified. He had not merely stopped in the middle of some piece of cheerful nonsense, but had stiffened, with a look of extreme embarrassment.

It was at Pete that Martha was looking. She was pale, but there were two small patches of vivid colour on her cheeks and there was a brilliance in her eyes and a light on her face that Robina had never seen there before. Perhaps for the first time she recognized the intensity of Martha's beauty.

Then she saw Sam thrust his way past Pete, take hold of one of the drawers of the wardrobe, drag it out with a gesture of unusual violence and stride out to the kitchen, saying, 'May as well smash up some more of this damn thing and start a fire. Where's the hatchet, Robina?'

She followed him out, aware as she went that neither Pete or Martha had moved.

Sam threw the drawer down noisily on the kitchen floor and looked wildly around him. 'Where's the damn hatchet?'

'I think it's just outside the back door,' Robina answered.

She was twisting Mr Darley's note round her fingers. It said that he had delivered five sacks of logs, at two shillings a sack. She had a curious feeling about the piece of paper. For some reason she felt that she must hold onto it. But perhaps it was only that at that moment she needed to hold onto something, even something so flimsy.

Sam looked outside. 'I can't find it,' he said.

'Oh, it's somewhere there.' She looked down at the twisted piece of paper, because she did not want to look at his face. 'I forgot to bring it in after I used it last night—I know I did. If you can't find it, I should think you could smash the drawer up with a hammer. Or just stamp on it!'

Something in her tone reached Sam and he stood still, looking at her with peculiar alertness. 'You know, it's just that I like Pete,' he said quietly. 'When she was talking yesterday I never thought for a moment she was talking about him.'

'Does it matter who it is?' Robina asked.

'But I *like* Pete.' There was dismay in Sam's voice.

'Can't you go on liking him?'

He did not answer. Then, in the silence as they stood there, someone pounded on the front door.

It made both of them start and Sam started to swear. But he was quicker than Robina in reaching the door. As his hand went out to it the knocking started again, sounding as if someone were using both fists to beat at the panels, in an agony of impatience. It might almost have been terror that was producing such furious knocking.

When Sam opened the door a tall thin woman dressed in black lurched forward and if Sam had not caught her she would have fallen.

For a moment Robina could not think who she was, though she knew that she had seen her before. Then, as the woman began to speak, she recognized her as Miss Woods, the Birches' housekeeper.

'For God's sake, come!' Miss Woods cried, clinging to Sam with both hands. 'She's done it, she's murdered the poor soul, murdered him—he's lying there in his blood! Oh, God, the sight of it!'

She opened her mouth to scream, but before the sound came her body went limp in Sam's arms and her face went white and empty.

CHAPTER 7

Sam carried her into the sitting-room. He laid her on the sofa. Both Martha and Pete stood watching him without speaking or making any attempt to help him, and one look at their faces told him that they had heard what Miss Woods had said.

But neither of them looked at Miss Woods or at Sam. It was at one another that they stared. Each face curiously mirrored the shock and incredulity on the other.

Then Pete said hoarsely, 'I'm going . . . I'm going to see what really happened.'

'I'll come with you,' Sam said.

'No!' Martha cried. 'Don't both of you go! Don't leave me alone with her!'

'Robina will stay with you,' Sam said.

As he said it he looked round, wondering why she was not in the room. He heard her running down the stairs.

Coming in, white-faced and breathing fast, she said, 'She made such a noise, I went up to make sure she hadn't woken them up, but they're all right. It can't be true, what she said, can it?' There was an attempt at re-assurance in her voice as she turned to Martha. 'It can't be true.'

'Pete and I are going to see,' Sam said.

Martha turned her dazed face towards him, clinging to his arm. 'As soon as you've seen, come back! Come back and tell me before—before you do anything else!'

He patted her hand clumsily, loosening its grip on his arm. 'As soon as we can,' he said, looking questioningly at Pete, who nodded. They went out together.

They got into the car without speaking. Sam turned it and had driven halfway to the Birches' house before Pete

56

said in calmer tone than might have been expected, 'We'll find it is true, I guess.'

Sam nodded. He did not look at Pete, but could see that he was leaning forward, peering tensely ahead as if there might be something to be seen before they reached the house.

'If it is,' Pete went on, 'there's something I . . .'

'Well?' Sam said as he paused.

'No,' Pete said, 'forget it.' He sat back, feeling in his pocket for cigarettes. He sounded fairly composed, but as his hand came up with a lighter in it Sam could see that it was shaking.

They found the gates at the entrance to the Birches' drive standing wide open and were able to drive straight up to the house.

It was a white house, showing up sharply in the darkness against a background of trees, a house of only moderate size, but in a big and beautifully tended garden, with smooth lawns that glowed emerald as the headlights swept across them. There were lights in several of the windows and as Sam and Pete sprang out of the car they saw light streaming out through the open door.

They went in. Both of them knew the house and went without hesitation to the door of the room where Douglas worked, ate and all but slept when he was alone, a room that had become like an outer shell for his nervous being. Martha had once said that he would have carried it about with him if he had known how.

Sam reached the door first and thrust it open. He was the first to see what was inside and he nearly slammed the door shut again to cut off the sight. But Pete, behind him, propelled him forward. They both went a few steps into the room, then stood still, side by side.

'God!' Pete said.

The room was a square one, with a high ceiling, from the centre of which hung a light in a milky glass globe. It was this hard white light that had been left on, shining on the scene before them.

The window was in the wall facing the door. It was a French window, opening onto a paved terrace and framed in curtains of grey velvet. The curtains had not been drawn. Near to the window was a big desk on which were a typewriter, an anglepoise lamp and some tidily arranged papers.

The fireplace was in the middle of a wall between the door and the window. There was a fire in the grate, but the rather excessive heat of the room came from a large radiator. On either side of the fireplace was an easy chair and beside the chair that had its back to the window was a low table with a tea tray on it.

In this chair, sprawled over one of the arms, was the body of Douglas Birch. Looking at him even from the doorway, there was no need to question for an instant that he was dead. A man could not live for long with a hatchet buried in his skull.

Sam never knew afterwards whether at that point he moved with intense rapidity or with leaden slowness. He was hardly aware of movement till he found himself at the desk, reaching for the telephone. What made him come fully to himself then was the feeling of Pete's hand gripping his own, wrenching it away from the telephone before he could touch it.

'Just a minute,' Pete said. 'Who's that call for?'

'The police,' Sam said. 'There's no need to call a doctor.'

'Didn't you promise Martha you'd let her know what had happened before you did anything else?'

'As a matter of fact,' Sam said, 'I did not and I'm not going to.'

'Then I am.' Pete picked up the telephone. 'What's your number?'

'We aren't connected yet. You won't get through.'

Uncertainly Pete put the telephone down again, just as a voice from the village exchange, sounding extraordinarily loud in the silent room, asked him what number he wanted.

Sam did not pick the telephone up again immediately. Details in the room were beginning to impress themselves on his mind, for instance, the undrawn curtains and the fact that only the central ceiling light had been turned on. Neither the standard lamp behind the empty easy chair nor the anglepoise lamp on the desk was alight.

But Douglas had been reading. A corner of the book, stained with his blood, showed between his body and the arm of the chair. Sam also noticed the broken teacup by the hearth and the spilled tea on the carpet.

He walked towards the fireplace. He had got over the first numbness produced by the sight of Douglas dead, and his brain seemed to be functioning with almost abnormal lucidity. He put his hand on the teapot and nodded.

'Stone cold,' he said.

Pete was watching him with a frown. 'What's on your mind, Sam?'

Sam did not answer.

Pete went on, 'Okay, call the cops. But one of us could go back to your house and tell Martha.'

'Let's give ourselves a minute to think.'

'What about? He's dead, isn't he? And it's murder. Go on and call the cops. I oughtn't to have stopped you.'

'No, but you did,' Sam said, 'and now I've started to notice things. And I'm wondering if you leapt to the conclusion, as I did, that Martha had murdered her husband. And then did you remember something about Martha's whereabouts?'

'The person to ask about that,' Pete said, 'is Robina.'

'I was coming to that. I'm going back to ask her while you call the police. Any objection?'

'There's just one thing,' Pete said. 'You're wrong that I leapt to the conclusion Martha did this thing. I never thought it for a moment.'

'Got any other suggestions—as to motive, I mean?'

'Robbery, most likely.'

'No signs of it, are there?'

'No, but we haven't looked around yet. Besides—' Pete came to a full stop.

'What?' Sam said.

Pete turned away from him. He started to look round the room and after a moment pointed at the sword that hung on the wall above the fireplace.

'There are plenty of things like that around,' he said. 'Some of them may be valuable and I wouldn't know if one was missing. Would you?'

'That isn't what you started to say,' Sam said.

Pete sounded as if he were trying to speak patiently. 'Oh, Sam, call the cops. This is their job.'

'That sword,' Sam said, 'is the one Douglas used last night when he tried to kill Martha—so she told us. It's a story that might help her now. Had you heard it, Pete?'

'No.' Pete said it expressionlessly, as if he were trying to cover up whatever feelings might have been roused by this information. 'It sounds to me as if you don't want to help her much.'

'If she did *that*,' Sam said, gesturing at the chair without looking at it, 'I don't think I do, particularly as . . .'

He was glancing around the room again, his forehead wrinkled, his light blue eyes hard and bright. He felt sure that he had missed something, that there was something there for him to see that would bring a new meaning into the scene, if only he could single it out from all the other less significant details.

He felt it as he sometimes felt it in the laboratory. The detail, the observation, the relating of two things to one another, the calculation that suddenly produced a pattern . . .

Pete was watching him and after a moment said, 'If I didn't finish saying what really came into my head just now, Sam, there are things you're keeping to yourself too. Now are you going, or shall I? Just so long as one of us does.'

'Yes,' Sam said. 'I'm going. With luck I'll be back before the police get here, but if they're here first I just went to make sure that Martha and Robina were all right.'

'Isn't that why you *are* going?'

'It's one of the reasons.'

Pete nodded and, as Sam went past him to the door, laid a hand on his shoulder. Sam gave him a swift look and caught an expression on Pete's beaky, usually good-humoured face that disturbed him a good deal. It was an expression of understanding, and at that moment Sam did not in the least want to be understood.

He went out. But he did not hurry to the car and before he left the house he heard Pete start to speak on the telephone.

Sam drove slowly back to the house. If he could have walked instead of taking the car he would have done so. But if he should later be asked why he had walked, he would not have found it easy to give a reasonable answer.

The truth was that something that he had seen in that room had scared him badly. As he related one thing to another, something had emerged that had given him a great shock.

He thought that Pete had perceived this. Pete's mind was quick and he was well equipped with intuition. His responsiveness to other people, which gave him a good deal of his charm, was based on a sometimes surprising degree of insight. Sam had noticed it in him before and had taken all the more account of it, perhaps, because he saw as much as he did of Denis Ovenden. Denis, far the more talented intellectually of the two young men, lived humanly, in blinkers. That would have made him this evening far the more reassuring companion.

Even so, Sam's main problem at the moment was not Pete but Robina. How much should he say to Robina?

He saw it as ill fortune now that he had never spoken to

her much about Martha. He had never wanted to do so and she had never seemed to require it. For both of them it had been easiest to treat that matter as closed. They had never spoken much of her first marriage either. In fact they had done very little exploring of one another's deeper experiences, arriving at an acceptance of one another on what suddenly seemed to Sam an extraordinarily small basis of knowledge. But was this the time to start rectifying that?

Getting out of the car, pushing open the gate, he had still not made up his mind just what he should do. He went to the door. As he reached it a sound caught his attention and he stood still and listened.

It was a sound of hammering. Realizing where it came from, he walked quickly round to the back of the house and there found Robina, in the patch of light that fell through the open back door, crouching on the doorstep, attacking one of the wardrobe drawers with a hammer and chisel.

She had already split most of the drawer into firewood. As she worked on what remained, she was muttering to herself in a tone of extraordinary ferocity, which she often did as she rushed from one job to the next, simply exhorting herself, so far as Sam could make out, to get on with it. She could always break it off in the middle and speak with perfect good humour to anyone else.

Breaking it off now as she heard Sam's footsteps, she stood up, hammer in one hand, chisel in the other, and said in a tone sharp with anxiety, 'It *is* true, isn't it?'

'Yes,' Sam said.

'Miss Woods came round quite quickly after you left. She told us the whole thing. At first she said it was Martha and it was awful. But I told her Martha had been here all day. And now it's Martha who's fainting and Miss Woods is looking after her and I felt I'd had about all I could take, so I came out here to get on with this job, then at least we can have a fire.' She held out the hammer and chisel. 'I've been using these things because I can't find that wretched

62

chopper. I know I left it out here last night. I suppose the children have hidden it somewhere. I oughtn't to have left it out, I know, but I simply forgot it . . . Sam, there's something I want to show you—'

'Just a minute,' he interrupted. Here was one of the things that he had noticed, one of the pieces of the pattern already dropping into its place. 'The hatchet, Robina. You left it out here—you're quite sure about that?'

'Yes. Why? Oh—' Her eyes opened widely. '*Oh no*, Sam!'

'I'm afraid so,' he said. 'I thought it was when I saw it there, and if it's missing . . .'

'I'll look again, I'll look everywhere,' she said. 'Perhaps I can find it. And I'll ask the children.'

'No, wait,' he said. 'Tell me something. Was Martha really here all day?'

They were both speaking hurriedly, in whispers.

'That's what I was going to tell you about,' Robina said. 'I wanted to show you this.' She put a hand into the pocket of her jeans and pulled out a piece of paper.

Sam took it. It was Mr Darley's note, by now rather crumpled, about the delivery of five sacks of logs.

'What's wrong with it?' Sam asked.

'I thought you might remember Pete picking it up,' Robina said. 'It was on the doormat, as if it had been pushed through the letter box. But if Martha was here when the man brought the logs, as she's supposed to have been, he'd have given it to her and she'd have put it down on a table or something, not just thrown it straight down on the mat.'

Sam nodded. He handed the note back to her. 'Well, keep it,' he said. 'Does she say she was here the whole time?'

'I haven't actually asked her,' Robina said. 'If she did go out, it was while I was over at the Ringroses', and when I thought of that I got so angry, because she'd said she'd stay with the children, that I came out here to chop up the wood. It didn't seem the time to badger her with questions. But then of course I started thinking . . . Sam, what happened when you saw Douglas this afternoon? Did he say he'd divorce Martha?'

These were the questions for which Sam had been waiting. 'I didn't see him this afternoon,' he said.

'But I thought when you left here with Denis—'

'That's just it,' he said. 'I drove Denis in to the lab and we got talking about work. And then I thought of some things I wanted to do myself, so I stayed on. The fact was, I didn't want to see Douglas and went on putting it off until I convinced myself it was too late. And on my way back I picked up Pete in the village and we went to have a drink. By then I'd decided that, whatever Martha said, I was going to keep out of her affairs, and I'd have told her that straight away when I got in if things hadn't started happening. Don't look so worried, Robina.' He brushed a hand against her cheek. 'This thing's a ghastly horror—that poor devil, Douglas, it's hardly to be believed. I'm thankful you didn't have to see it. But you and I aren't going to get involved in it. Understand?'

'I wonder if we can help it.'

'Well, there's something I'm going to do about it right away,' he said. 'I've got to get straight back, I told Pete I would. But I'll telephone Edna Swinson on the way—there's a call box outside the post office—and ask her to come and collect Martha presently. I think she'll do it.'

'But you can't do that, can you?' Robina said. 'The police will want to see her.'

'Yes, but after they've seen her. Think what it'll do to Miles and Miranda if Martha stays on. They'll hear a good deal about it all anyway—that can't be helped. But think of the emotional buffeting they'll get if she's here. We've got to shift her.'

'Only it seems mean . . .'

He gripped her suddenly by both arms. 'Robina, don't feel sorry for Martha! Don't waste your feelings on her, don't get entangled with her! Keep clear of all this, use all you've got to keep clear of it. Now I'm going back. Tell Martha I've been, but that I had to get straight back to meet the police. As soon as I can, I'll come back again.' He gave her a hard kiss on the mouth, turned and walked off quickly.

He drove fast now. He drove to the little post office in the middle of the village, fumbling for pennies in his pocket as he jumped out of the car.

In the call box his voice was suddenly hoarse as he asked for Edna Swinson's number. He heard the telephone begin to ring. He heard the repeated burring sound going on and on and thought that no one was coming to answer it. But at last the ringing stopped and he heard Iris's voice saying hullo.

It was not Edna that he asked for then, but Denis Ovenden.

CHAPTER 8

Robina had gone back to the sitting-room, taking the firewood with her. She found Miss Woods standing in the middle of the room and Martha in a chair, lying back limply with her eyes closed.

Miss Woods had her eyes on the door. As Robina came in she took a step towards her.

'That was Dr Mellanby, wasn't it?' she said.

'Yes.' Robina went to the hearth and knelt down in front of it. 'He went straight back, to be there when the police arrive.'

'I know I ought to have sent for the police myself, instead of running out like that,' Miss Woods said. 'I'm ashamed of myself now. But I couldn't have made myself stay in that house another minute after finding what I did.'

She had told Robina, while Sam had been gone, how she

had returned to the house after going to the pictures in Blanebury with her married sister, as she did every Thursday. She had gone to Douglas's study to collect the tea tray, which she always left ready laid for him in the kitchen, so that he had nothing to do but boil the kettle and make the tea. Until she went into the study she had noticed nothing amiss, except that the front door was ajar, and this, she had thought, meant only that Douglas had perhaps gone out to post a letter, or might even be roaming about somewhere in the garden.

'Even though it was dark,' she had said, 'he'd sometimes walk up and down on the lawn, thinking to himself. He'd finish his writing, have his tea, go for his walk and then sit down by the fire again with a book and a glass of sherry till dinnertime. Only sometimes he didn't seem able to settle down again, so he'd go out in the garden and walk up and down. I'd think when I saw that, "He's too much alone," I'd think, "he ought to go out and see his friends or have someone in for a drink, like in the old days," but he didn't seem to care for that any more. He's seemed just to want his own company lately, and that isn't good for a man, you know, Mrs Mellanby, specially one that uses his brain all the time, like him. There hasn't been one party in that house since that New Year party, and that's nearly a year ago now. But in the old days we had lots of nice parties, as Dr Mellanby will tell you . . .'

She had talked on and on, in the state of uncontrolled garrulousness that sometimes follows shock. Now she was more her normal self again, a quiet, rather stiff, anxious woman.

'I'll be going back,' she said. 'I'll have to tell the police all about it, and most likely they'll want to know why I came here instead of going for Sergeant Fox. I know that's what I should have done, but I lost my head.'

'What will you do tonight?' Robina asked. 'You can't stay in that house.'

'I'll go to my sister's. And thank you for your kindness, Mrs Mellanby, and Dr Mellanby too.' She glanced at Martha. 'I'll tell the police, like you said, that she's been with you all day. If it weren't for that . . .' She shrugged her thin shoulders and went out.

Robina struck a match and held it to the crumpled newspaper in the grate. As the flames rose up round the sticks and the logs that she had heaped there, she stayed kneeling where she was, trying to draw some immediate warmth from the fire into her shivering body.

The shivering had started outside, at the time when Sam told her what had become of the lost hatchet. Or had it started a little later, about the time that Sam told her that he had not seen Douglas that afternoon? She could not really remember. What did it matter? Sombrely intent, her grey eyes watched the movement of the flames, which threw a red light over her thin face and small, crouching figure, though no heat seemed to reach her, even when the dry wood had begun to crackle.

This would not do, she told herself. The way to stop the shivering was to get busy. Murder or not, there was a meal to be cooked, a meal for four people, since Sam would probably bring Pete back with him. Only heaven knew when anyone would feel like eating. That, naturally, made it harder. She had meant to grill the piece of steak that she had bought in Blanebury yesterday morning, before coming out to the house. But she had bought only enough for Sam and herself. So it would have to be eggs. In an emergency one can always eat eggs. Thank God for the hen . . .

'You think I did it, don't you, Robina?' Martha said.

Robina started and looked round.

Except that she had opened her eyes, Martha had not stirred. Her small head lay back against the cushions as if it were too heavy for her to lift. Her forehead looked moist and under her wide cheekbones her cheeks were sunken.

'You did go out,' Robina said.

'I didn't.'

Robina felt in her pocket and brought out Mr Darley's note. 'I found this on the mat when I got in. If you'd been here to answer the door when he brought the logs, he'd have handed it to you, not pushed it in through the letter box.'

'I know—if I'd answered the door.'

'What d'you mean?'

Martha drew a long breath, pulled herself upright in the chair and thrust her fingers through her short, dark hair, pushing it away from the forehead that looked so damp.

'It's going to be difficult to explain,' she said, 'and I think you're the last person who could understand it. I'm not at all like you. You'd never cower behind a door, feeling terrified of having to open it to a strange man, would you? You wouldn't mind being alone in a house with just two young children upstairs. You're a reasonable, tough sort of person, who'd say to yourself that the number of females who actually get assaulted in empty houses by men who come knocking at the door in the dark is far less than the number who get killed crossing the road in broad daylight, or swallowing fishbones, or something. That's the sort of argument Sam used to try on me. "But look at the statistics," he'd say. Good God, statistics! Would anyone but a scientist ever dream that you can affect the human nervous system by statistics?'

'Then you didn't answer the door?' Robina said.

'Of course I didn't.'

'But when you heard him throwing the logs into the bunker and knew who it was—'

'For heaven's sake! Don't you understand at all what I'm trying to tell you? It was dark outside, I was alone . . . And it isn't all my fault, you know. It's the way I was brought up. My mother would never stay alone in a house, and when my father went away, which was quite often, because he was an actor and spent a good deal of time on tour, an aunt of mine always used to move in to stay with us, or we packed up and went to stay with her, and they used to talk about their fears, as if it would have been almost indelicate not to have them.'

'But haven't you ever tried to get over it?' Robina asked.

'Oh, what would be the use?'

'Well, just in case you *had* to face it sometime. But the point is now, you didn't go out.'

'No.'

'I wish I knew whether or not to believe you.'

'I know you aren't going to believe me,' Martha said. 'I'm sorry about it, because I like you and you've been good to me, and I think we just might have managed to be friends, if Sam would let us. But he won't.'

'What d'you mean by that?'

Martha made an impatient gesture, as if she found Robina's mind intolerably slow. 'You'll see, he'll prevent it,' she said. 'Men like to live their lives in separate compartments and they don't like the compartments to overlap. He's never told you much about me, has he?'

'Why should he?'

Martha stared at her for a moment, then gave a half-smile. 'You're right, really. There isn't any reason. I can see you're going to make a success of your marriage, which is more than can be said of me. Poor Douglas, for some months now I've almost hated him, and of course he hated me, though he didn't know it. I don't like to think of that now. Yet it's ticking away at the back of my mind already that I'm free. Free from his awful, possessive hatred! Isn't that horrible —to think that so soon?'

'I didn't know Douglas very well,' Robina said thoughtfully. 'If I'd hated a person, I suppose I'd think much the same. But I might try not to show it—for my own sake. D'you know where the—the weapon came from that killed him, Martha?'

Martha shook her head.

'It's our chopper—the thing I couldn't find when I

wanted to chop up the wood—or so Sam thinks.'

Martha's limp body suddenly grew rigid. She did not speak, but it was clear what thoughts and what fears were racing through her mind.

Robina added, 'I left it just outside the back door last night. I chopped up some wood out there to make a fire before the Swinsons came, and I left it there. I don't know when it disappeared.'

'But then it could just have been stolen—I mean, by anybody,' Martha said. 'I thought at first . . .'

'That it must have been someone who was in this house?' Robina said. 'I think it must have been, you know. Miranda and Miles were in and out of the house all day, and I don't think anyone could have got to the back door without being announced to us with shrieks of excitement.'

'That's just another nail in my coffin then—and perhaps was meant to be,' Martha said. 'And I suppose I'm not really helping myself now by acting as I am. I ought to have gone home with Miss Woods—*home*, what a word for it!— and played the bereaved and distracted wife before she managed to say too much against me. But I'd hoped, after last night, never to see the inside of that house again!'

'What really happened last night?' Robina asked.

'Just what I told you.'

'Sam doesn't believe it.'

'Sam!' Martha said derisively. 'Sam hates me. Hadn't you noticed it? And he isn't even honest with himself about it. Sam's vanity is that he's a tolerant, understanding, superior being, much stronger and wiser than most other people. He's got his passions in hand, he believes, and can afford to be half kindly, half contemptuous about the feelings that wrack other people. Only it isn't fair of me to talk to you like this about him. I'm sorry.'

'Go on with what you were going to say,' Robina said in a level tone.

'I was going to say, Sam thinks he understands Douglas.

He thinks he's a mild, harmless sort of man, very quiet and quite good-natured. But d'you think he's ever read a single thing that Douglas has written, or thought about what they mean? Have you?'

'Well—no,' Robina said.

'I had to read them all,' Martha said. 'What's more, I had to *be* them all. I had to be all those horrible Restoration or Jacobite or Regency heroines of his, with flashing eyes and heaving bosoms and always throwing crazy tantrums but then yielding adoringly in the end. And in a way I suppose that's why he stood as much from me as he did. His heroes always took an awful lot from those frightful women. But by degrees I found the yielding part growing more than tiresome. And as soon as Douglas began to feel that he hadn't really got power over me he became a hysterical bully. Those are the real facts that Sam's never understood at all.' She gave a mocking smile. 'I wonder how Sam got on with him this afternoon? I wonder what Douglas said to him?'

'Sam didn't go to see him this afternoon,' Robina said. 'He thought better of it and stayed in the lab.'

'He . . . ?' For a moment Martha looked as if she had been given a blow. Then she stood up. 'I suppose I'd better screw up my courage and go back to that house after all,' she said.

'I don't think I should,' Robina said. 'In the circumstances, I'd remain in a state of shock.'

Martha gave her a startled look. Robina got up and hurried out of the room.

She went to the kitchen. She tipped the Ringroses' brussels sprouts into a basin, put it in the sink, ran cold water over them and started to trim them with swift, fierce cuts from a sharp little knife.

Not that she had any intentions of cooking the brussels sprouts that evening, but she had to give herself a job of some sort to do. It had taken all the self-control she had to listen to Martha explaining Sam to her, all the more because she thought that what Martha had said, in a one-sided way, was somewhere near the truth. Robina had found herself resenting beyond all reason the fact that another woman should have this knowledge of him, and should dare to discuss it with her.

At the same time, it would have been the worst ignominy possible to betray the strength of this feeling. All of which, of course, was rather contemptible, when there were far more important things to think about. For instance, whether or not Martha had been telling the truth when she said that she had not stirred from the house that evening. And who had taken the hatchet? And why, when Sam said that he had not seen Douglas that afternoon, had he certainly been holding something back?

But none of these questions, even with the help of the brussels sprouts, was particularly calming and on the whole it was a relief when Sam and Pete returned to the house, even though they brought several policemen with them.

Robina did not know what Martha told the police that evening. They interviewed her by herself in the sitting-room, and stayed, it seemed to Robina, a surprisingly short time. But it was while this interview was proceeding that Edna Swinson arrived. She had come on her bicycle, red-cheeked and panting, wearing her usual old raincoat, her grey hair wind-blown, and with what looked like a pair of bronze doorknockers clamped to her ears.

She, Sam, Pete and Robina sat in Sam's study, among the piles of books that had not yet found their way onto the bookshelves.

'Of course I'll take her back with me,' Edna said in answer to Sam's question. 'All this business of people wandering in and out while you're trying to get settled—it's all very well, but I know what a nuisance it is. And my experience is that if you don't keep on and on, when you first move into a house, until you're really straight, you somehow get stuck at a point and then you may stay like that for months.'

'It isn't because of that,' Robina said. 'It's because of Miles and Miranda.'

'I know, dear, but still the other's important,' Edna said. 'The only problem, as far as I'm concerned, is Iris. As soon as she heard what had happened she said, "Martha did it." I said, "You mustn't say that sort of thing, you don't know anything about it. So far as I'm concerned, poor Martha is just someone in terrible trouble until I know different." I said, "Look at all the trouble that was made for poor Denis because people leapt to conclusions when they hadn't any evidence." I said, "I'm bringing her home and you can be making up the bed in the end room while I'm gone."'

Pete reached out and squeezed one of Edna's hands. 'That's my girl! I've been telling Sam it was robbery and I guess you'll be on my side. But the guy's stubborn. He insists on suspecting his friends and neighbours.'

'Was anything stolen?' Edna asked.

'That's the point,' Sam said. 'Talk of stubbornness. Miss Woods has been round the house with the police and she says there's nothing missing. But Pete won't accept that as evidence.'

'She may not know everything.' For some reason Pete had coloured. 'Would she know how much money Douglas had in the house?'

'She thinks so,' Sam said. 'He was a creature of habit, and went to the bank and cashed the same amount every week. It seems it can all be accounted for.'

'The steadiest guy in the world changes his habits once in a while,' Pete said.

'And the chance burglar knows just which day he did it —and steals our hatchet for his purpose?'

'What's that?' Edna asked. 'Your hatchet?'

Sam told her about its disappearance.

Edna's red cheeks did not grow any paler as she thought this out, for this was something of which they were not capable. Instead their colour stood out more hectically, as if it had been daubed onto her face.

'But that means—'

'Let's stop talking about it!' Robina broke in violently. 'It doesn't do any good. We all know next to nothing. Those little hatchets mostly look exactly alike and in the morning we may find Miles and Miranda have been stalking deer with it in the orchard or something. Or Miranda may even have hidden it under her pillow to defend herself against Martha's three-footed witch. If those two are about, you never want to take anything for granted.'

'That's true,' Sam said. 'But it's a suggestion that can keep till the morning. We don't want the police waking them up tonight to ask them questions.'

'Have you told the police about its being missing?' Robina asked.

'Yes.'

'And?' She was going to ask him if he had told them about Mr Darley's note and the delivery of the logs, but meeting his eyes, she thought she saw a warning in them, and instead of finishing the question, tapped her pocket, into which he had seen her put the note. He understood what she meant and gave a very faint shake of his head.

Edna did not notice this interchange, but Pete did. He gave Sam a frosty look and got up and went to the window, standing there staring out at the darkness.

The whereabouts of the hatchet, when she had last seen it, was the only question that the police asked Robina that night. She had to show them where she had left it and for a while they searched for it in the garden with their torches, but presently gave it up and left. While they were doing this Sam, with their permission, drove Edna, Martha and Pete to Blaneford.

When he returned he found Robina in the kitchen, grilling the steak, which after all was going to be enough, since there were just the two of them.

He stood still in the doorway, sniffing. 'It's an extraordinary thing,' he said, 'a moment ago I'd have sworn I couldn't eat a thing, and now I've just realized that I'm ravenously hungry.'

'I'm nearly sick with hunger,' Robina said. She went to the cupboard for two plates and put them on the rack above the stove to get warm. 'And I'm sick for a little peace and quiet, and I'm sick to be on our own.'

He came in and stood behind her, laying his hands on her shoulders. 'We are on our own now,' he said.

'Thanks to Edna. She's a dear,' Robina said. 'I'd like to be that sort of person, I mean the sort of person you can always count on.'

'You don't do so badly,' he said.

'No, my good nature wears out after a bit. You can't think how glad I was to see them all go. Oh, Sam—' She turned to him, leaning her head against him. 'Let's not go on talking about it. We're on our own now for the very first time in this house—let's just talk about—about the paint and the garden and ourselves.'

For a moment he said nothing. Then he kissed her lightly on the forehead and moved away and sat down at the table. 'All right,' he said. 'About the colour of the paint for the woodwork outside . . .'

But there was a note in his voice that Robina recognized. It was what she thought of as the protective note, the understanding note, but to which Martha had given a much less flattering description. She would have said that Sam had begun to play that stronger, wiser, superior person, who was gentle with the weaknesses of others because he saw himself as being without them.

It was not true, of course. All the same, Robina knew that if she had not spoken just as she had at that moment and made just that appeal to him, he would have told her something that was on his mind, easing himself of a burden which he had now decided to carry alone. Also she knew him well enough, or thought that she did, not to argue, for the time being, with this decision.

CHAPTER 9

In the morning Miles and Miranda discovered a rosebush. It grew close to the low stone wall that encircled the garden and was entwined with some blackberries, so that the single creamy rose that had opened that morning looked as if it had flowered miraculously on a bramble thicket.

The children fetched Robina to admire the marvel. She had to leave the breakfast washing up, go with them through the wet grass and weeds, step in amongst the trailing brambles, getting scratched about the ankles, and pick the rose for them. It was a little, old-fashioned rose, its outer petals almost white, those at the centre yellow as butter.

'Does it smell?' Miranda asked excitedly, holding out her hands for it.

'Not much, I'm afraid.' Robina extricated herself from the clutching thorns of the brambles. 'But it's very pretty. We'll have to see if we can save the bush.'

'How do we save the bush?' Miles asked.

'Oh, we'll clear the brambles away and we'll prune it and manure it.'

From the other side of the wall a voice said, 'My dad feeds our roses with blood.'

Robina turned round with a start.

A boy of about seventeen, seated on a bicycle, had propped himself against the wall, with one elbow resting on the top of it. She did not know how long he had been there. He was a round-faced, red-haired boy, with a scrubbed and wholesome look about him.

He went on, 'He cleans it up off the floor with the sawdust

and boils it up in a tub and waters the ground with it. Our roses do lovely.'

Robina's mind cleared. It had been suddenly paralysed by a ghastly vision of some neighbour in the quiet little village of Burnham Priors performing dreadful animal, or even human, sacrifices for the sake of his roses. This vision was close enough to the kind of dreams she had had in the night to have been, for an instant, hideously compelling.

'I know, your father's Mr Lawley, the butcher,' she said with relief.

'That's right,' the boy said. 'And I called in to ask if you'd like us to bring you your meat. We deliver Wednesdays and Saturdays. I could bring you in something tomorrow morning, if you'll give me your order.'

Robina considered it for a moment, decided the suggestion was a good one and ordered a joint of beef. The boy brought a notebook out of his pocket and wrote it down.

'Sirloin, four pounds, English . . . "I sometimes think that never blooms so red a rose—" as where the Sunday sirloin bled.' He grinned. 'Okay, Mrs Mellanby, you shall have that.'

Robina was still laughing in a slightly bewildered way as he pushed off on his bicycle and rode off down the road.

'Mummy,' Miles said, 'can we feed the rose now?'

'Well no,' she said, 'we'll have to clear the ground first and—' She stopped as a thought struck her. 'We might cut some of the brambles away now,' she went on. 'Only we'll need some shears, and we haven't got any. I wonder if we could manage with the hatchet—the one I was using the day before yesterday to chop up some firewood. Do you know where it is?'

Both children shook their heads. They stood there waiting to be told where it was. Robina had not honestly expected anything else, but the loss of the faint hope that she had built on the possibility that they might have concealed the hatchet for their own private purposes brought on a sharp despondency against which she had been struggling ever since waking.

She went in search of Sam. He was furiously at work upstairs with coils of electric wiring.

'They don't know where it is,' she said.

'No,' he said, without needing to be told what she was talking about.

'So that means . . . Oh hell!' She turned to go downstairs again, but paused to tell him about the butcher's boy who quoted poetry when he took her order.

Sam looked up with a smile. 'Misquotes, which shows even more confidence. We live in a changing world.'

'It's certainly a change having someone call for orders,' Robina said. She started down the stairs. She was near the bottom when the doorbell rang. 'I don't suppose that's the coal, however.'

It was not, it was the police.

A man whom they had not seen the evening before, a man not as tall as Sam but so much wider, thicker, heavier, that except when they were standing side by side it was inevitable that he should seem the bigger, a man in a navy-blue suit and a raincoat, introduced himself as Detective Inspector Morton and told Sam and Robina that he would not keep them long, but that he had heard something about a hatchet that was missing.

They took him into the sitting-room, and Robina told him about the loss of the hatchet. He went over with her a list of the people who had had an opportunity to take it. Besides Martha, Sam and herself, there were Edna Swinson, Iris Swinson, Pete Hillman, Denis Ovenden and Mrs Booker. The inspector asked her some questions about Douglas's visit to her, and made sure that she had used the hatchet after his departure, so that he at least need not be on the list.

'I wanted to be sure of that,' he said, 'because it seems he made a murderous attack on his wife that evening, and if he'd had some such thing in his mind already and taken the hatchet himself—well, it would have opened up the field.'

'Talking of that attack . . .' Sam said.

'Yes, Dr Mellanby? I'm assuming that Mrs Birch told you about it when she came here.'

'Yes,' Sam said. But he stopped there, looking embarrassed.

The inspector went on. 'Perhaps you've some doubts about that attack. In that case it may interest you to know that Miss Woods, the housekeeper, witnessed it. That's to say, she saw Mrs Birch run out of the house and saw Mr Birch follow her to the door. He had a sword in his hands and he shouted after her, "I'll use it—don't think I don't mean it—if I have to, I'll use it!" Miss Woods swears those were his exact words.' The impersonal voice sounded as if he did not mind whether or not they were listening to him, making it plain that he offered them no opinion on what he was telling them.

Sam tried to challenge him. 'And what do you think that means?'

'What would you say it meant, Dr Mellanby? You knew Mr Birch better than I do.'

Sam shook his head.

'When she arrived here,' Morton went on, 'did you think she was scared?'

'Yes,' Robina said. 'I thought so.'

'And you put her up for the night and she stayed with you all next day, I believe.'

'Yes,' Robina said again.

'The whole day? Didn't she go out at all?'

'She went out into the garden. And . . . well, I went out myself for a time, so I can't say for sure what she did then, but she'd told me she'd keep an eye on the children while I was gone. I'd just put them to bed, and—and I suppose she did what she promised.'

'What time was it that you went out, Mrs Mellanby?'

'I think it was about half past five. I went over to the Ringroses' to return the basket that Mr Ringrose had left here in the morning. I was gone for about an hour.'

'So until half past five you know Mrs Birch didn't go out.'

'Yes.'

'Between say four and five o'clock . . . ?'

Sam moved his feet suddenly. It was only a slight movement, a small change in their position, but it made Robina aware of the tension in his long, slight body.

She asked, 'Is that when it happened, Inspector?'

'Some evidence points to it,' Morton answered.

'The medical evidence?' Sam asked.

'As it happens, the medical evidence is rather uncertain,' Morton said. 'You may have noticed when you went in, the room was unusually hot. And there's a curious fact about that. The setting of the thermostat that controls the central heating had been altered. That could mean various things. But its effect might have been to delay some of the normal post-mortem effects, so that it's even more important than usual to consider other evidence.' He turned back to Robina. 'Between four and five o'clock . . . ?'

'Oh yes, Mrs Birch was here then,' Robina said. 'She was telling stories to the children. If she—if she did go out at all, it was later.'

'The other evidence . . . ?' Sam began.

'You saw the room yourself,' Morton said. 'Miss Woods says she touched nothing in it, except that she turned on the light. The central light. When she went in, the room was in darkness.'

'I see,' Sam said. It was as if what the inspector had said supplied him with a piece of information that removed some doubt in his mind.

'There's an interesting thing about that light,' Morton said. 'There were no fingerprints on the switch except Miss Woods's. None at all.'

'And the motive?' Sam said.

The inspector turned his head, so that he appeared to be speaking directly to Sam. Until then, even when he had been answering Sam's questions, he had seemed to be speaking to Robina.

'It's early to say,' he said, 'but it isn't impossible that the motive was robbery. Yet there's another possible explanation of certain facts that have come to light.'

'What was taken?' Sam asked.

'If anything, a rather large sum of money. Yesterday morning Mr Birch went to his bank in Blanebury and cashed a cheque for five hundred pounds. We haven't been able to find that money in the house.'

Sam frowned nervously. He moved his feet again. 'Who would have known he had it?' he asked.

'That's a very important question. Yet one must never rule out chance. Someone may have made a far bigger haul than he expected. Murders have been done for fantastically small sums. If it weren't for the fact that your hatchet had been taken it would be a good guess that someone broke in, looking for what he could pick up. In the normal course of events, you see, the house would have been empty at that time. Miss Woods always went out on a Thursday afternoon, and Mr Birch generally went for a walk. It's true Mrs Birch might have been at home, but she'd been in London for some weeks and it might not have got around yet that she'd returned.'

'But does the sort of man who breaks into empty houses, looking, as you say, for what he can pick up, take to murder?'

'Not often.'

'That's what I thought.'

'But there's always panic.'

'Birch was sitting in a chair, reading,' Sam said. 'He hadn't even got up. And he was killed from behind.'

'Quite right.'

'So you don't, in fact, believe in that explanation.'

81

'Perhaps it isn't the most probable.'

'And it's a matter of some importance to find out who knew that Birch had cashed a cheque for that sum that morning.'

'Well, not necessarily.' Morton glanced at Robina, then back at Sam. 'As I said, there's another possible explanation of the disappearance of that money. It isn't, you see, the only considerable sum that Birch cashed in recent times. During the last few months he's made several withdrawals, not of sums quite as large as this one, but of two hundred pounds, three hundred pounds—sums like that. And on each occasion he insisted on having them in one-pound notes.'

A startled interest showed on Sam's face. He leaned forward. 'You're thinking of blackmail.'

'It's a possibility.'

'But a blackmailer doesn't murder his victim. That's to say, not unless—'

What stopped Sam in the middle of his sentence was the sound of footsteps in the hall. He swung round to see who was there. Whoever it was stopped at the door, which was ajar, knocked on it and gave a diffident cough. Then, her presence sufficiently announced, Mrs Booker pushed the door further open and put her head in.

'Excuse me, Mrs Mellows,' she said, 'I know it isn't my day for coming, but I thought, what with everything, you might do with some extra help, so if you like I'll get ahead with the washing up in the sink, unless you don't want me here. You needn't be afraid to say, only if it'd be a help I've got the time to spare.'

'That's very good of you, Mrs Booker,' Robina exclaimed.

'It's just I've got the time to spare,' Mrs Booker said.

'Thank you very much indeed.'

'I'll get on with the washing up, shall I?'

'If you would. I started it, but I—I was interrupted.'

'That's how I thought it'd be.' Mrs Booker closed the

door and they heard her tramp off to the kitchen.

Robina suddenly beamed at Morton. 'And I thought, after yesterday, she probably wouldn't come again!'

He was caught unawares by her delighted smile and actually smiled back, which for an instant transfigured his unrevealing features. Robina thought that he probably had a wife too and that his own private peace and happiness might often depend on the reliability or lack of it in the domestic help. But fortunately he mistook Robina's meaning, assuming that she had feared that the murder might have kept Mrs Booker away. This misunderstanding saved Robina's possibly having to enter on irrelevant explanations about the meeting between Mrs Booker and Denis Ovenden.

He returned to the theme of blackmail. 'As you say, Dr Mellanby, the blackmailer doesn't murder his victim, unless the worm turns. Then the worm can be a danger. But it's difficult to make that fit the facts as we know them at present. Mr Birch cashed that money in the morning, as if he had every intention of continuing the payments. The only thing is, he cashed it in five-pound notes this time, which is different from the other times. And as you pointed out, he was sitting peaceably reading and having his tea when he was killed. That doesn't encourage one to form a picture of, say, a quarrel breaking out between him and the blackmailer, a sudden refusal to pay, a threat to risk his own security and go to the police with information against the blackmailer. All the same, it seems likely that blackmail fits into the picture somehow. But not certain. We have to remember that. Of course not certain.'

Soon afterwards he left. Before leaving, he asked Sam for an account of his movements during the previous afternoon, and Sam told him what he had told Robina, that after driving Denis into the research station he had gone to work in his own laboratory for a while, then had driven back to Burnham Priors, picked up Pete in the road and gone to the Lion and Lamb for a drink.

Sam went with Morton to the gate and, as he drove off, walked slowly back into the house, looking at the ground in front of him. His shoulders were more slouched than usual and his lower lip was caught under his teeth. He came into the sitting-room and stood like that in the middle of it, looking as if some thought had arrested him there, unaware for the moment of his surroundings.

Robina had drawn her feet up into the chair and was digging her small pointed chin into her knees. 'But whatever could anyone blackmail Douglas *for*?' she exclaimed.

Sam did not appear to have heard her.

'Sam!' she said.

He looked towards her, but she was sure he was not seeing her. She started to repeat her question.

He interrupted her. 'It struck me at the time as a bit odd. He was so positive about it, when there wasn't any evidence for it. And it turns out he was right.'

'The inspector?' she said, not quite able to follow his meaning.

'No,' he said. 'Pete. Last night he suggested straight off that the motive was robbery. And he started to say something about it, but stopped himself and said something else about our not being able to tell if any valuable ornaments or what not were missing. And . . . Damn! Why did I have to think of that?'

'What?' Robina asked quickly.

'Only that he *was* there, in the road.'

'I don't think Pete's a blackmailer.'

'Of course not.'

'Well then?'

'Oh, I don't know what I'm getting at myself,' he said. 'It's just that Pete seemed to know something. That's all. And I could be wrong about it.' He kicked at a table leg with one foot. 'Quite wrong,' he muttered. 'As we could have been wrong about that scene between him and Martha. There's something about that that doesn't seem to fit.'

Robina uncoiled her legs and stood up. 'We didn't tell that man anything about Martha and the logs,' she said. 'I suppose that was the right thing to do.'

'I should think so.'

'Because there isn't really much to tell, is there?'

'No.'

'And he wasn't really interested in what she was doing as late as that.'

Sam started to say something, but stopped as Mrs Booker came into the room.

She was holding a tea cloth in one hand and several forks and spoons in the other. As she spoke, she rubbed at them, one by one.

'Excuse me interrupting, but there's a thing I feel I've got to say,' she said. Her bright, candid eyes were full of worry. 'It isn't that I suppose you think I'm a person who listens at doors, and I didn't listen, and if I hadn't been coming just to tell you I was here and ask should I stay or not, I'd not have heard it. But I did hear it, and so I thought I'd better tell you I did, in case of things being said. That gentleman who was here, for instance, the one who was talking about the blackmail, I don't know what he thought. So I thought I'd tell you about what I heard, I mean about the blackmail. That's the same as demanding money with menaces, isn't it?' She looked at Sam questioningly.

He nodded, trying to sort out from what she had said whether she had come merely to apologize for having overheard part of a private conversation or whether there was something else she was trying to say.

'That's what I thought,' she said.

'D'you mean you know something about it, Mrs Booker?' he asked.

'Not *know*,' she said. 'Not actually *know*. And I don't like gossip, but still it's easier to talk to you than the police, and I thought you could advise me if it's my duty to go to the police, which I don't like to do if I can help it. It's just a

question, you see, of where the Ringleses get the money to
buy television and washing machines and all. There's been
a lot of talk in Burnham about that, and if there's going to
be talk about blackmail, that's what a lot of people are going
to say. And then there's the other thing too that Miss Woods
said to me in the road this morning. She said, "It's such a
small thing," she said, "I don't know whether to bother the
police with it, but there it is." So I said, "I'll ask Dr Mellows
what he thinks, because he's a clever man with letters after
his name," I said, and she said, "Do, Mrs Booker. ''

She looked expectantly at Sam. His glance at Robina was
a signal for help.

She said, 'What did Miss Woods say to you, Mrs Booker?'

'It was just about the ice,' Mrs Booker answered. 'The
ice cubes being missing, and the tea cloth being used. She
said, "I filled the trays in the fridge up with water that
morning and I put two clean tea cloths on the airer, and
when I come back, one of the cloths' been used and Mr
Birch never does any washing up in my kitchen," she said,
"and four or five ice cubes are missing. It's such a small
thing," she said, "I don't know whether to bother the police
with it." So I said, "I'll ask Dr Mellows, Miss Woods," and
she said, "I wish you would, Mrs Booker."'

CHAPTER 10

Sam took refuge in saying that this was a matter that he
must think over with some care and discuss with his wife.
Mrs Booker thanked him and went back to the kitchen.

Sam arched his eyebrows at Robina, grinning faintly. 'I
consider myself a reasonably domesticated type,' he said,
'but I don't feel sure I've grasped the inwardness of all that.'

'It's quite simple,' Robina said, 'but I haven't the least
idea if it's of any importance. As I understand it, the

point that's worrying Miss Woods is that she feels some unauthorised person has been mucking around in her kitchen. If they hadn't, the ice tray in the fridge would have been full of ice cubes and the tea cloth would still have been clean when she got back from the cinema. And from her knowledge of Douglas's habits, she feels sure that that person can't have been Douglas. Apparently he was capable of boiling a kettle and making his own tea, if she left everything ready for him on a tray, but that's as much as he'd tackle.'

'And what d'you make of this unauthorised person?' Sam asked. 'What was he or she doing in the kitchen?'

'The ice being missing suggests someone was mixing a drink.'

'Yes,' Sam said. He was looking at her in a strained, expectant way, as if he thought that she would have more to say. 'That's what I thought.'

'And the tea cloth,' she went on less certainly, 'that suggests . . .' She stopped and considered it. 'Were there any glasses in that room?' she asked.

'No.'

'Then it suggests that whoever had the drink washed up the glass after he had it.'

'Why?'

He snapped the question at her and Robina realized that it was not because he needed an explanation of what had happened but that he was pressing her on to see if she would arrive at some conclusion that he had reached before her.

'I suppose,' she said, 'it was because he didn't want to leave any sign behind that he'd been there.'

'The murderer?'

She started to say that she supposed it must have been, but in the middle exclaimed, 'Oh no, that doesn't fit! Look, I can imagine that someone who'd just committed a murder would make a grab at a whisky bottle and drink half of it off, but I can't imagine him going out to the kitchen, getting ice out of the fridge and carefully mixing himself a highball . . . Oh!' The word, as she heard herself speak it, gave her a shock. She saw now the conclusion to which Sam had been leading her. 'Oh *no*!' she said.

He said nothing.

'No,' she repeated, 'it's as impossible that Pete had anything to do with the murder as it is that Denis killed Booker and left him to die in a ditch. If you won't believe that of Denis, you can't believe this of Pete.'

'I didn't say I believed it,' Sam said. 'I just wanted to see if we'd both get the same answer to the sum. And since we have, it's probable that other people may get it too. I think that means we'd better advise Miss Woods to say nothing about all this for the present—at least till I've had a chance to talk to Pete.'

'But what I said still stands,' Robina said. 'No one, not even Pete, would bother with ice in his drink at a time like that.'

'Doesn't that depend on whether he had the drink before or after the murder? Look at it like this—'

At that moment the telephone rang.

It was so unexpected, they were both so sure that the instrument was mute and useless, that they were as startled as if they had suddenly discovered that there was someone in the room with them, listening to all that they had said.

Sam grabbed the telephone up. A voice from the exchange informed him that it was now connected and could be used. He muttered thanks. Putting it down again, he put both hands to his head.

'All this,' he said in a carefully controlled tone, 'is not good for one's powers of concentration, damn them. As I was saying . . .' He gave Robina a blank look. 'What was I saying?'

'About the drink.'

'Oh yes. Well, if you think of its happening like this, you'll see how Pete fits in. Suppose he went to see Douglas—'

'When?'

'I don't know. Sometime in the afternoon. And Douglas said, "Have some tea, I'm just going to have mine," and Pete said, "No, thanks," and Douglas said, "Have a drink then," and Pete said, "Sure," and Douglas said, "With or without ice?" . . . You see, if you remember the night before last, Pete was the only one who had ice in his drink, and it was probably one of those people who took the hatchet.'

'Or Denis, or Mrs Booker, or Ringrose—no, Ringrose never went near the back door.'

'Denis wouldn't have had ice, and Douglas wouldn't have offered Mrs Booker a drink—a cup of tea, possibly, but not a drink.'

'And you're still remembering that Pete may have known something about the money and that you found him wandering around in the village. And there's something else you can add to it. Of all the people we've mentioned, he's about the only one who might have thought of washing up the glass he'd used. Only in that case I don't think he'd have been such a fool as to dry it on a clean glass cloth.' There was a slight edge on her voice.

Sam came to her and slid his arms round her. 'You're getting angry with me.'

'A bit,' she replied.

'But I'm not trying to work up a case against Pete. I've only interpreted a set of facts in a way that I think they may easily be interpreted by other people. I don't say that I've interpreted them correctly. All the same, I think that the facts themselves are important and that our friend the inspector ought to know them. But I'd sooner he didn't know them till I've talked to Pete.'

'Will you tell Mrs Booker that?'

'Suppose I tell her that I'm still thinking deeply about them, and that meantime I advise her to avoid precipitate action.'

'All right. But, Sam—' She rested her hands on his

shoulders. 'I think you do believe that Pete was in that house sometime yesterday afternoon.'

'What if he was?'

'Yes, what if he was? That's what I was going to say.'

'I'll go and look for him now, shall I? The only thing is, there's all that wiring trailing around upstairs . . .'

'Oh, leave it!' she said.

When he had gone she stood in the middle of the sitting-room and looked round. She had the feeling that by now at least one room in the house should be past the stage of looking half furnished, unlived-in, disorganized. If everything about this move, from the arrival of the furniture a day early onwards, had not gone wrong, she would probably have had the whole ground floor straight by this time.

At the moment the laying of the carpet was the thing to get on with.

The carpet, rolled up, was in a corner of the hall. Robina took hold of it and pulled, pushed, heaved and jerked it into the sitting-room. By the time she had achieved this she was panting and talking to herself about the abominable habits of rolled-up carpets, which are much heavier than they look, do not remain rolled up when they should, and send up clouds of dust into the eyes of anyone who tries to wrestle with them. She was still talking to herself and pushing all the furniture into the corners of the room, so that she could spread the carpet over the floor, when Harold Ringrose came into the room.

He had been brought to the door but abandoned there by Mrs Booker, who did not think it part of her job to announce visitors. He saw what Robina was doing and quickly went to the corner of the carpet opposite to the one at which she was tugging, gave it a firm pull, which flattened out most of the wrinkles in it, gave it another pull, which made it lie straight with the floor boards, stepped across it and took hold of it at another point, pulled it once more so that one edge of it reached precisely to the edge of the hearth, then stood up, brushing the dust off his hands.

'That's awfully good of you, Mr Ringrose!' Robina exclaimed. 'It would have taken me ages to manage that by myself.'

The drab little man gave a complacent nod. 'Properly speaking,' he said, 'you ought to have put it down before you brought all the furniture into the room, then you wouldn't have had such a job. Stands to reason.'

'Of course it does,' she said. 'But it was packed right at the far end of the van and was almost the last thing to come into the house.'

'Ah, trust them for that,' he said. 'No one likes to do a proper job of work any more. If there's a right way and a wrong way to do a job, trust them to pick the wrong way. You ought to vacuum it next, you know, before you move the furniture back onto it.'

The remark slightly damped Robina's gratitude. It was smug, she thought, it was irritating. Naturally she had intended to vacuum the carpet next. She found herself remembering that Mrs Booker had accused this small, wiry man with the greenish eyes and the forced smile of being a blackmailer, and also that she had no idea of why he had come to see her. He had not been at all glad to see her the evening before in his own home.

'Let's just pull a couple of chairs out of the corners,' she said, 'then we can sit down without having to look right across the room at one another.' She looked round vaguely. 'I think there are some cigarettes somewhere.'

'Thank you, I don't smoke,' he said. But he pulled two chairs onto the carpet and pushed them near to one another. 'It's true what I wanted to say isn't just the thing to shout at the top of one's voice. I'm afraid it's something that may distress you, Mrs Mellanby. Of course you may be aware of it already, which will save me some trouble, but in case you aren't, there's no need for us to take everyone in the house into our confidence, is there?'

There had been no change in his voice while he was speaking and the smile had stayed on his face, but it seemed to Robina that the harsh lines that ran from his nostrils to the corners of his mouth had deepened, as if with the tension of some hidden excitement.

'I don't think I understand,' she said, hoping that she did not show how much she shrank from him.

'No, of course you don't, not yet,' he said. 'But I'll put it very simply. That's always best in the long run, stands to reason. It'd be a pity to be interrupted before we did understand each other, wouldn't it? So long as we know where we are with one another, then we're both all right. You know your husband's safe and I know I'm not going to lose by—well, considering his welfare, as you might put it, which is what I naturally should prefer to do. Dr Mellanby's the sort of man I admire. He's a scientist, he's modern. He's not one of these fossilized types—'

'Mr Ringrose!' Robina was sitting bolt upright in her chair. 'What are you trying to say to me?'

He gave an embarrassed shrug. Robina at once felt a horrible certainty that the embarrassment was wholly false, and that really he was burning with pleasure.

'It's only a little thing, really,' he said. 'Nothing for you to worry about yourself. It's just with his telling the police he didn't go to see Mr Birch yesterday and me seeing him come out of the house, I'm put in a rather curious position. Of course I could keep what I saw to myself, but that means I might be taking a bit of a risk—depending on what really did happen in that house, if you see what I mean. So I thought we might make matters square by some slight compensation for the risk I'm running—nothing out of the way, of course. I understand that what with buying a house and all you might find it a little inconvenient—'

'Inconvenient!' Robina's eyes, unusually wide open so that the long lashes cast no shadow on them, were blazing. She was cold inside, but instead of looking scared she looked furious. 'You're quite right that we should find it *inconvenient* to pay you blackmail. We're neither as rich nor as easy to scare as Douglas Birch. You must not count on our help to buy your refrigerator.'

The smile disappeared from his face. His lips parted slightly, the lower lip jutting forward in a way that gave his face a look of scornful malice. 'Now *I* don't know what *you're* talking about, Mrs Mellanby,' he said. 'I said we could keep this simple, didn't I? Let's not bring in a lot of other things that one or other of us doesn't understand. I'm talking about Dr Mellanby being in the Birches' house yesterday afternoon, that's all. His being there when he told the police he wasn't.'

'And I'm talking about refrigerators, and television sets, and washing machines!' Robina was not handling this in the way that she would have liked to think herself capable of handling it. She would have liked to be able to stay cool and controlled, telling Ringrose, with great dignity, to leave at once. But this was beyond her. She had a feeling that for the first time in her life she was in contact with something almost completely evil, and she did not know what to do about it but lose her temper.

He must have seen this, for he stood up. 'Perhaps it'll be best if I let you think it over—and discuss it with your husband, naturally,' he said. 'I'd do that, Mrs Mellanby, I really would. Just calm down and think it out.'

'There's nothing to think out,' she answered. 'You're a blackmailer who doesn't even know his job. My husband was at the research station yesterday afternoon.'

That brought the smile back to his face. 'That's what he told you, is it?'

'And now get out!'

'At the research station? And you may even believe it. In that case, naturally, you'd find it hard to understand my point of view.'

'Get out!' Robina said.

'All right, all right. But think it out and then drop in and see me when you're ready. Only don't take too long about it, because this is the sort of thing you can't hold back from the police for very long without getting into trouble. You at least understand that, don't you? You understand you'd better not take too long.' He went to the door.

Robina followed him, feeling that she must watch him until he was out of the house, out of the garden, out of sight, and that, if necessary, she would stand at the gate, snarling and with her teeth bared, to make sure that he did not come back.

But at the gate he came face to face with Denis Ovenden.

Robina immediately called to Ringrose to stop. 'Now,' she said, 'we can settle this! Then we can ask the police to drop in on you, Mr Ringrose. Denis—' He had stopped in the gateway, looking at her in a puzzled way, seeing her excitement. 'Can you tell this man where Sam was yesterday afternoon?'

Denis turned his square, heavy face towards Ringrose. He looked at him as if he were something exceedingly small and far away, which he could not quite distinguish against his background.

'Yesterday afternoon, Robina?' he said. 'Well, we were here for a time, weren't we? I mean, I came to lunch, if you remember.'

'Of course I remember,' Robina said. 'And afterwards?'

'Well then, I was going to help Sam with the books, but we got talking instead.' He gave an apologetic laugh. 'I don't think we did an awful lot about the books, actually.'

'After that,' Robina said.

'Well, he drove me in to the research station, and we got working.'

'Oh,' Ringrose said, his hand on the gate, 'so you're all in it, are you? You got working, did you? In the same room all the time?'

Denis looked questioningly at Robina. His eyes, that

usually showed the uncertainty, the anxiety of the very shy, were quite clear now. 'D'you want me to answer that?' he asked.

She nodded emphatically.

'Well, we don't work in the same room,' Denis said, 'but next door to each other, and I went in to consult him several times in the afternoon, and he came in to see me just before he left. That was about a quarter or ten to six, I think.'

Ringrose's mouth twisted in the same way as it had earlier, the lips parting slightly, the lower lip jutting forward. 'So you've got it all fixed up between you, that's what you think. Fixed up to tell a pack of lies. And you think your lies'll be believed, rather than what a chap like me has to say, because people call you doctor, and write letters after your names and pay you a lot more than you're worth. Well, we'll see about that. I gave you your chance, Mrs Mellanby. I could have saved you a lot of trouble. Everyone here knows the motive Mellanby had for killing Birch, and I can put him on the spot at the time of the murder—right—on—the —spot! And I'm not going to waste any time doing it now. You had your chance.' He swung the gate open and walked off.

Robina stood at the gate, looking after him. She was trembling, though she did not know it. The sense of an evil that remained almost tangible as long as the small, swiftly walking figure was in sight made her feel that she had to stay there to ward off the menace of it from all that was precious to her. But Denis put his hand on her arm and gave her a slight push which brought her to herself. They went into the house together.

Robina immediately pounced on her handbag. She took out two pound notes. 'Denis, be a darling and go to the Lion and Lamb and bring me back something to drink,' she said. 'Anything that's strong—or I think I might start crying or be sick or something.'

He took the notes. All his usual shyness had come back.

He looked down at them, twisting them in his fingers. 'Did I say what you wanted me to say?' he asked.

'Of course,' she said.

'I wasn't sure—I'm not sure now, it was the right thing to say. He was trying to blackmail you, wasn't he? And now he'll go to the police. Is Sam here, by the way?'

'No.' The sense of cold inside her had come back. 'He wanted to talk to Pete. Why d'you want him, Denis?'

'To tell him I think—I think he's making a mistake.' He looked up at her. 'It isn't that I mind backing him up—it isn't that. He stood by me about that blasted accident, and I'll stand by him over this in any way he wants. But I think —I mean, I don't think—that is, I think he'd have been wiser to stick to the facts and not try to show he was in the lab when he wasn't. I mean, all sorts of other people may have looked into the lab during the afternoon and seen he wasn't there, or they may have seen him around somewhere else. Like that frightful little man—he saw him, I suppose. I'd have said all this to Sam on the telephone last night when he rang me up, but Iris was there in the room and I couldn't. So I came over to say it this morning, I mean, to ask him if really it wouldn't be better to stick to the facts— though if I'm all wrong about that and there are reasons for what he's done that he couldn't tell me, I don't mind going on saying what I've said already. I really don't, Robina. Don't think I'm worrying about that.'

She had forgotten about wanting to cry or be sick, but she still felt cold. The cold had spread right through her. 'What are the facts, Denis?'

'Why, that he drove me in to the lab, then drove straight off again. Now I'll go and get this drink. I'll be back in a few minutes.'

CHAPTER 11

The worst part of it all for Robina at that point was in admitting to herself that she was not surprised. It was a shock, yes, but not a surprise. Ever since Sam had told her, the evening before, that he had not gone to see Douglas in the afternoon, something in her had been waiting to be told that this was not true. She kept remembering too how Martha had said that Sam was a liar.

The shock was a complex one. She did not try to analyse it. Instead she fetched the vacuum cleaner, plugged it in and went to work on the carpet. She went at it in a kind of fury, as if this would decontaminate it from the touch of Ringrose.

Held at bay in her mind was a terrified sense of loss. She was not sure what she had lost, or how completely, but the feeling was both dreadful and familiar, taking her back several years to those hours when she had waited in the hospital, after Brian's accident, not surprised but wholly unable to believe that he must die.

Perhaps something in her mind had been lamed at that time, leaving it with an inability to take calamity seriously. Her body, her nervous system could take it seriously, making her shiver with the chill of illness. But her mind insisted that nothing disastrous had happened or was about to happen to her. If she kept busy, did not try to tackle problems that were beyond her and took for granted that all would come right in the end, somehow the bad time, the unbearable time, would pass.

By the time Denis returned with a bottle of whisky she had lost her desire for a drink but, because she had sent him for it, thought that she must have one. Fetching glasses, she poured out two drinks, gave one to him and lit cigarettes for them both.

With her glass in one hand and her cigarette in the other, she walked restlessly up and down the cleared space of carpet. She assured Denis that she was quite sure that, whatever had made Sam ask him to lie on his account, his reasons would turn out to be good ones. Denis watched her nervously.

'I know,' he said. 'Naturally. I know there's nothing to worry about. I mean to say, I didn't mean to worry you, Robina. I didn't realize Sam hadn't said anything to you yet about that call to me. If I had, I'd have kept my mouth shut.'

'I think he was going to tell me about it last night,' Robina said, 'then he saw I was tired and . . . Well, I'm an awful fool. I said, "For God's sake let's not go on talking about it all night!" So—so of course he didn't.'

'But there's nothing for you to *worry* about,' Denis said. He often found conversation with other people, particularly people in tense emotional states, so difficult that he did not listen too carefully to what they said but, concentrating on what he thought essential to communicate to them, would reduce it to a few simple sentences, which, if necessary, he would go on repeating until there was no possible doubt left that they understood him. 'I mean, you needn't worry about Sam's being mixed up in this murder. And I'm awfully sorry I brought it all out just now. It really isn't because I mind backing him up, if that's the best thing to do. It really isn't. I don't want you to think that of me, Robina.'

'He'll have to tell the police the truth,' she said. 'Whatever his reasons were, that's the only thing to do.'

Denis raised his voice slightly. 'But I *will* stick to the story if that's what he wants. I'm not going to let him down. You know what Sam did for me after that accident, don't you? The accident when Booker was killed and everyone said I'd done it. I easily might have too—that was the worst part of it. I felt almost as if I had. I was quite mad that night. I don't know what happened to me. I've never felt like it before or since. I didn't even know I was the person who could act like I did that night in Douglas's house. And if Sam hadn't helped me then and believed that I hadn't killed that poor devil, I don't know what I might have done. So I don't want you to worry. You mustn't worry. That isn't what I meant at all.'

Robina stood still, looking at him. She had only half heard him. 'I'll have to get hold of Sam somehow,' she said. 'I could telephone—yes, *telephone*! It's working! Though I don't know where he's likely to be. I'll try his lab, and if he isn't there I suppose there's just a possibility that he's at Edna's, if he went looking for Pete.'

'If he did he won't find him,' Denis said. 'Pete went out quite early this morning.'

That was what Edna Swinson also said when Robina, having failed to find Sam at the research station, spoke to her a few minutes later.

'He called in here, looking for Pete,' Edna said, 'but he didn't stay. I wanted him to stay, because there was something I wanted to talk over with him. It's about—' She paused, as if she were taking a swift look round to make sure that no one would overhear her. 'It's about Martha. If you don't mind, I'll pop over and tell you about it. It's something she said to me this morning, when I took her up some coffee after the police had been here. I'm keeping her in bed—that's easier for me as well as for her. She's in a queer state, I don't understand it. It's as if . . . Well, I'll tell you when I see you. I'll just put some lunch on a tray for her, then I'll pop over. Don't worry, I shan't stay long and get in your way.' She rang off.

Robina told Denis what she had said.

'In that case I'd better push off,' he said. 'If Sam wants me I'll be in the lab. And you'll tell him what I said, won't you?'

Robina shook off her anxiety enough to pay some real attention to him at last. She saw how harassed and bewildered he looked, watching her, she thought, rather as if she were some dangerous compound that might explode in his face.

'I will, Denis,' she said. 'And thank you—thank you very much for everything.'

'You do understand what I—I mean that I don't mind—'

'Yes,' she said. 'But Sam will have to get this straightened out with the police. Even if it weren't for that man Ringrose, I think he'd have to do that. I don't think any of us are good enough liars to do anything else.'

Denis looked relieved. 'I know I'm a rotten liar,' he said. 'I think so slowly.'

When he had gone Robina went out to the garden to call the children in for lunch. By the time Edna arrived she had them settled at the kitchen table, under the eye of Mrs Booker, who had said that she could stay on for the afternoon, if it would help.

Robina, foreseeing many more discussions at which the presence of the children would be a great embarrassment, accepted the offer thankfully. She made a sandwich and some coffee for herself, then returned to finish cleaning the carpet and to straighten the sitting-room.

This was still not done when Edna propped her bicycle against the wall of the house and came in. Accepting some coffee and a cigarette, she repeated that she would stay only a moment. But if it was Martha about whom she wanted to talk, she showed no signs of coming immediately to the point.

She began by saying, 'Oh, God, Robina, what a business it is, having a daughter!' She puffed out a cloud of smoke and leant back, stretching out her muscular legs and planting her feet, in their sensible shoes, well apart. 'You simply don't know. Well, not yet, anyway. I never had to bother about

Iris until the last couple of years. Of course she was always falling in love with all my lodgers, Sam and that nice boy who got a job in Australia last year, and Bill Mason, who wanted her to marry him, and whom she fell out of love with the moment he asked her, so that the poor boy went and got himself a job in Leeds or Sheffield or some ghastly place like that. But it never upset her, if you see what I mean. She just seemed to enjoy herself. But now, heaven help her, she's grown up, and I don't know what to do about it but get rid of all my young men and turn my house into a home for old people—which I've nothing against, in a general way, except that it would be twice the work.'

'What's she been doing?' Robina asked.

'Just suffering,' Edna said. 'Suffering, moping, pining—and snarling at me half the time, as if I ought to be doing something about it. And probably I ought, only I don't know what.'

'It's because of Denis, isn't it?'

'Denis?' Edna said, looking surprised. 'No, it's Pete. And Pete doesn't know she's walking the earth. Oh, he's very nice to her. He takes her to the pictures sometimes, and dancing, and lets her feel she's an attractive girl, all of which is rather out of Denis's range. But it doesn't mean a thing. Pete, you see, has had his head a bit turned by another character, and now that we've got her in the house ... whew!' She gave a lopsided grin.

'I'd no idea,' Robina said, 'none at all—about Pete and Iris, I mean.'

Edna looked at her shrewdly. 'Then you had some idea about Martha? Not that I suppose it's serious, but that doesn't help Iris. And the child's got no self-control at all. She made the most awful scene last night, after we got home with Martha, and this morning Pete got up at crack of dawn and went off without any breakfast, so that he needn't see either of them, and I must say, I don't blame him. That's mainly why I've persuaded Martha she's had such a shock, she's got to stay in bed. I mean, so that I can keep her out of Iris's hair. You see, Iris accused her to her face of murdering Douglas. I was really ashamed of her. But I'm so sorry for her too, my dear, so frightfully sorry.'

'I'm sorry too,' Robina said. 'If I'd had any idea of this, Martha could have stayed here.'

'That wouldn't have been too good either,' Edna said. 'And to send her off to a hotel would have been just heartless. No, I'll handle it somehow.'

'You know, I thought Iris's troubles were all on account of Denis,' Robina said. 'I can't say I felt I knew what they were, but I always felt there was something wrong between the two of them.'

'That's all over ages ago, if there ever was anything,' Edna said. 'She rather mothers him and pushes him around, as a matter of fact, which seems to suit him, because outside his work he's an utter child. It's true she gets madly impatient with him, but what mother doesn't? And recently it may have been partly because he was around too much, when she'd sooner have had Pete to herself. And then sometimes I've wondered . . .' She paused, 'The fact is, I'm gossiping too much, but sometimes I've wondered what she really believed about that accident. Before it, perhaps she was a bit in love with Denis, then after it, for a time, she seemed almost to hate him, and then by degrees she developed the mothering business. But that brings me round to what I came to talk about. I'm sorry I've been such a time getting to the point—which is that Martha told me this morning that it was Douglas who killed Booker.'

Robina gave a startled exclamation. But immediately afterwards she felt that she ought not to have been startled. 'Somehow,' she said after a moment, 'it's rather easy to believe it.'

'I know,' Edna said, 'that's what I felt. In fact I don't know why no one ever suggested it before, except that no one seems to have thought that Douglas might have taken his car out that night. The party was in his house, after all. There was no reason for him to go out. But Martha says he did, after all the guests had gone. She says he wasn't actually drunk, but he was in a very wrought-up mood about something, and he was gone for about half an hour. Then when he came in he wouldn't go to bed, but sat up all night and drank most of a bottle of whisky by himself. Later, when she heard about Booker, she asked him if he'd killed him, and he went quite wild, threatening all sorts of things if she ever spoke of it again. She says he never actually admitted killing Booker, and she'd no proof of it, but she'd no doubt of it whatever. And that's why she's lived with him as little as she could since then. She said it felt like living with a murderer. If it's all true, I must say I've more sympathy than I had with her before. I used to think she treated Douglas shockingly, but really it was a rotten position for her to be in, and in her way she's been surprisingly loyal to him.'

'D'you think it's true?' Robina asked.

'Well, you know there's some evidence that he was paying blackmail to someone, don't you?'

'Yes, the police told us that.'

'Well, don't you think that this was probably the reason? If someone saw him drive out that night, or even saw the accident, they'd have a terrible hold on him.'

Robina nodded thoughtfully. 'Yes, and he might easily have been seen—by someone who lived nearby. When did Martha find out about the blackmail?'

'Only this morning, from the police. And that's what I wanted to tell you about—I mean, the queer state she's been in since they told her. She's been crying her eyes out and saying, "If only I'd known, if only I'd known—" just as if his being blackmailed somehow excused him in her eyes. She's really an awfully odd girl. I don't understand her at all. What d'you think it means?'

Robina was starting to say that she had no idea, when a key clicked in the latch of the front door. 'Here's Sam,' she said. 'You'll tell him all this, won't you?'

'You tell him,' Edna said. 'I'll go home. I've been interrupting you long enough.'

But Robina insisted on her repeating her story to Sam, while she herself got him some lunch. Running out to the hall, she asked him if he had managed to find Pete, but he shook his head. As he went into the sitting-room and greeted Edna, Robina went to the kitchen, where she found Mrs Booker with Miles and Miranda, all three of them seated at the table, deeply absorbed in a game of beggar-my-neighbour. Mrs Booker looked up with a smile. Making sandwiches and some more coffee for Sam, Robina found herself marvelling at the luck that had brought this kind and sturdy old woman to help her.

She wanted to tell her so, but the game of beggar-my-neighbour had reached an exciting phase and she decided not to interrupt it. Returning to the sitting-room, she wondered if Mrs Booker guessed that her own tragedy might have some relation to this new tragedy that had come to the village.

Edna was finishing telling Sam her story as Robina came into the room. 'There, that's all, and now I'll really go,' she said. 'I just wanted to tell you what Martha told me and about the queer way she acted when she heard about the blackmail. It's almost as if—well, as if it upset her much more than the murder. Of course that may just have been a sort of delayed reaction. I dare say one oughtn't to try to make too much sense of it. Can you make any sense of it, Sam?'

'You say it happened after the police had been to see her?' he said. 'Perhaps they said something that frightened her in some way, that she hasn't told you about.'

'Frightened?' Edna said. 'Come to think of it, that might have been it.'

'But if it was Douglas who killed Booker,' Sam said, 'and that fact's known by someone besides Martha . . .'

'Well?' Edna said as he paused.

He shook his head again. 'I don't know. I was just wondering if in fact it mightn't be known by more than one person, and if so, what that would mean.'

'I see,' Edna said, though she did not look as if she did. 'Well, goodbye, my dears. If there are any more developments I'll let you know, but I admit I hope very much there won't be.'

'Developments!' Robina exclaimed as soon as she had gone.

Sam, biting into a sandwich, looked at her sharply. She looked back at him, feeling the cold, the fear, spreading through her again, the dread of something about to happen, of a step that had to be taken that might send her plunging down and down into complete disaster.

Sam saw it all in her face. He said, 'Robina, what's happened?'

'That man Ringrose has been here,' she said. 'He told me he saw you coming out of the Birches' house yesterday afternoon. He knows that you told the police that you hadn't been there. He tried to blackmail me.'

He waited, as if he thought that she would have more to say. She waited too. Sam stood up. He went to the window and stood there, looking out at the bare trees across the road, bending before the November wind.

The set of his shoulders, the way his arms hung at his sides, seemed more relaxed, more at ease than when he had come into the room, as if he felt it a relief to have been found out. He turned again and faced her.

'It's quite true,' he said, 'I did go there. I lied to try to give myself some time, because I think I may be arrested for Douglas's murder.'

105

CHAPTER 12

Because of the way that he looked at her as he turned back to face her, and because of the way that the tension seemed to have gone out of him, Robina knew that Sam wanted to talk to her. Yet he did not seem to know where to begin. He fidgeted with lighting a cigarette, with getting himself a drink, and insisted that Robina should have one too. He pushed chairs about on the half-cleaned carpet. Robina began to fear that he was having second thoughts and that what he would end by telling her would turn out to be only a part of the truth.

Perhaps recognizing this, he started abruptly. 'You've got to believe me. I'm going to tell you how things looked when I walked in there last night with Pete. I'll try to keep it simple. Look . . .' He took a pencil out of his pocket and fumbled around till he found an old envelope. 'Here's the room.' He drew a square. 'Here's the fireplace, in the middle of this wall . . . Here are the two armchairs, on either side of the fireplace—this is the one that Douglas was in, the one with its back to the window . . . Over here, *next to the other armchair*—that's the important point—is a standard lamp. There's a table with a tea tray on it next to Douglas's chair. There's a teacup on the floor and some tea spilled on the carpet. And Douglas was reading—the book had slipped down between his body and the arm of the chair . . .' He handed his diagram to Robina. 'Now what do you make of it?'

She looked at it, frowning. 'Was there only one teacup?' she asked.

'Yes, but that isn't the point at the moment. Think about the lamp'

'It wasn't on?'

'No, but that doesn't much matter either. The real trouble in that whole setup is this—Douglas was reading, and he'd sat down to read *with his back to the window*, not close to the lamp.'

'That means then that it was still daylight when he was killed.'

'That's exactly it! And what time does the daylight fade at the moment? When d'you normally turn on the lights?'

'About half past four, I think.'

'So Douglas was murdered before half past four. That's the whole meaning of the scene, you'd say?'

'Isn't it?'

'Yes—only I was there at half past four, and Douglas wasn't murdered.'

He crumpled the envelope in one hand and threw it at the fireplace, where it lay on top of the ashes of last night's fire that had still not been cleared away.

'He hadn't been murdered before I got there, and I didn't murder him while I was there,' he said. 'But that scene says that it must have been one or the other.'

'Then something about that scene must be all wrong,' Robina said. 'Someone changed something deliberately to give it that meaning.'

'Yes.'

'Mightn't they have moved his body from one chair to the other?'

'I don't think so. There was a lot of blood, you see.'

'Then—well, perhaps he wasn't reading. Perhaps the murderer pushed the book onto his lap. Perhaps the murderer had been sitting in the other chair and they'd just been talking to each other. Perhaps they were having tea together and—Sam!' In sudden excitement she started forward to the edge of her chair. 'That tea cloth that had been used! Surely it must have been used to dry the other cup, the cup that wasn't there. Someone wanted to make it look as if Douglas was killed an hour or so before he really was, so he washed up the cup he'd drunk out of himself, put that book on Douglas's knee and turned out the lights. That made it look as if Douglas had been having tea by himself and reading while it was still daylight.'

'I think you must be right about the book,' Sam said, 'though I don't see how anyone is ever going to prove it. But I don't think you're right about the tea.'

'Why not?'

'Because if that tea had been made after I left, I think, in a room as hot as that was, the teapot would still have been warm when Pete and I got there, which it wasn't. No, I think Douglas must have had his tea earlier than usual, that's to say, before I got there the first time. Then he must have taken the tray out to the kitchen and the murderer must have brought it back, to make things look as if Douglas had been having tea alone and reading, as you said. That cloth . . .' He gave a slight shake of his head.

'You're still thinking of Pete, aren't you?' Robina said. 'You think Pete was there sometime in the afternoon and had a drink.'

'I'm not thinking of Pete as the murderer.'

'But if he went to the trouble of washing up his own glass after he'd had his drink, doesn't it suggest just that?'

'If he did.'

'Who else would do it?'

'Someone who knew I'd been there before him, and who wanted me incriminated, rather than Pete.'

Robina gave a shudder. 'I know you mean Martha,' she said. 'I don't believe it, Sam. It isn't—it just isn't possible.'

'Why isn't it?'

Robina had her reasons for what she had said, but meeting Sam's eyes just then, she found herself wondering what she would feel like if ever, when it was of her that he was thinking, she were to see that expression in them. The thought drove out of her mind what she had been about to say.

'How you hate her!' she said. 'You do, don't you? She was quite right.'

'Did Martha tell you that?'

'Yes, last night.'

'And you believe her.'

'Isn't it true?'

'Perhaps it is. Yes, it is. Because I'm afraid of her. I told you that myself didn't I?'

Robina nodded.

'But I didn't tell you why, did I?' Sam said.

'I thought—I thought at the time you were afraid of her attraction for you.'

He gave a laugh that had no amusement in it. 'That's over a long, long time ago, Robina. Or it seems a long time ago.'

'But then why . . . ?'

'It's a rather difficult story to tell. It hasn't much to do with my having been in love with her, and next to nothing to do with Douglas having taken her from me, though perhaps those things give a rather sharper edge to my feelings than they'd have otherwise. But for one thing—she tried to stop me marrying you.'

She looked at him in astonishment.

'Oh yes,' he said. 'But not because she wanted to get me back.'

'But then . . . ?'

'Then why? That's the puzzle, isn't it? Why do some people do things like that? I suppose because of the feeling of power it gives them. Or that's as near as one can get to explaining it. A pathological state, you can call it, only that doesn't make it any easier to deal with.'

'But what did she do?'

'Tried to plant the idea in my mind that you weren't in love with me, and that all you really wanted—Oh, God, Robina, I don't want to talk about it! But I'll tell you that there was a point when she nearly, damned nearly, succeeded. Then something you said, or did—I don't even remember quite how it happened—drove all those things out of my head.'

'That all I really wanted—was someone to look after me and the children,' Robina said softly.

His face flushed. He ground out a cigarette and immediately reached for another.

'She really did?' Robina said. 'She really tried to make you believe that?'

'She did. She didn't go at it quite directly, she was fairly subtle about it, but that was what it came to. And it's curiously easy to accept the idea that, if one's been found wanting by one woman, one isn't likely to be loved wholeheartedly by another. That's to say, for a time it's easy.'

'But she didn't make you accept it!'

'Not quite. No, my dear, not quite. But there are some other things she's made various people believe which have caused a good deal of unhappiness. Douglas, for instance. She never let him forget me or get used to the idea that everything between her and me was really over. And then there was Denis.'

But Robina's thoughts had not followed him when he started to talk of Douglas and Denis. Slipping down onto the floor, she knelt close to him and slid her arms round his neck.

'One's so silly about all these things, always,' she said. 'Just when one needs the most sense, one's silliest. D'you know that at first it didn't seem possible that you could love me after Martha? I thought I'd have to work on you for a long, long time!'

He pushed her a little away from him, looking into her face.

'Yes,' she said, 'that's what I mean. Looking at us both like that, side by side, how could you really . . . ?'

'So help me,' he said, 'I don't think I ever looked at her like that.'

'And the odd thing about that is that I believe you,' Robina answered.

He gave a laugh and suddenly kissed her softly on one side of her forehead. 'For one thing,' he said, 'Martha would never have tried making up to me with a smudge on her face.'

'Was that kiss on the smudge?'

'Plumb on top.'

'Then it would be shockingly unresponsive of me to get rid of the smudge, wouldn't it? . . . What were we talking about?'

The laughter died out of his face. 'About Martha, Douglas, Denis . . . damn them all! Need we go on with it?'

'What were you going to say about Martha and Denis?'

'Only that she was the first person who told me and Edna and one or two other people that it must have been Denis who killed Booker. And she knew all the time who it was.'

'At least that showed a certain loyalty to Douglas.'

'It was unforgivable. She could have said nothing, that would have been understandable. But there'd have been no excitement in that, there'd have been no drama.'

'And you really believe that she murdered Douglas and deliberately tried to incriminate you?'

He got up and poured himself another drink. 'Just now you said that wasn't possible. Why isn't it possible? We know that Douglas was killed later than it appears, we know that she almost certainly left the house while you were out, we know that she persuaded me to go and see Douglas, we know that she's the sort of person who'd try to involve someone else if she could.'

'But how could she tell beforehand that I was going to go out? How could she tell how long I'd stay out? That's what I meant when I said it wasn't possible,' Robina said. 'Perhaps she could have killed Douglas—I suppose that could just have happened. If she left the house immediately after me, killed him and rushed straight back, she'd have been taking a great risk, but still, it might just have happened—particularly if she hadn't actually planned it. But to have stayed on in that room, thinking out just what she ought to do about the lights and the curtains and the book and the tea tray, when she knew that I might have got home already—it doesn't make sense, does it?'

Sam started to walk up and down the room. 'No,' he said, 'it doesn't.'

'What I've been wondering,' Robina went on, 'is whether she didn't go out on some impulse, rush over to see Douglas —and find him dead. That would explain, if one can convince oneself she's really callous, that little scene when we all came in. I mean the way she looked at Pete. She was— well, triumphant.'

'I've been doing my best to forget that scene,' Sam said. 'One shouldn't jump to conclusions about the looks on people's faces. I jumped to conclusions then, because of what she'd been telling us. But except that Martha was excited about something and Pete a bit upset, I don't feel in the least sure any more what it meant.'

'What was Pete like when you picked him up in the village?'

'Quite normal, so far as I could tell.'

'Would he have been if he'd been to the Birches' house and found Douglas murdered?'

'There's no reason to suppose he'd found Douglas murdered. I only think he'd been there or was going there when I met him. That was about six o'clock. The murder might have happened after that.'

'But then . . .' As she grasped the implications of what he had said, she gave him a bewildered stare. 'But then you weren't coming from the Birches' house when you met Pete.'

'No, I was coming from Blanebury.'

'But I thought . . .'

'I'm sorry if I haven't made it clear. What I did that afternoon was this. I drove Denis back to the lab, then went to see Douglas. I think I got there about four and left about half past. I told him about Martha's coming to us the night before and wanting me to go and talk to him about a divorce. He was in a queer mood, quite friendly really, but in a way amused, as if he thought Martha had been making a fool of me in some way, which was rather how I felt myself. He told me there was nothing to worry about, that Martha was going to America with him, that he knew she would go. We ended up talking about quite other things. Then I left and drove back into Blanebury.'

'Why?' Robina asked.

'Just that I'd had an idea—nothing to do with Douglas or Martha. As a matter of fact . . . Wait a minute!' He went out of the room.

She heard him go to the front door and open it and the sound of his quick footsteps outside the house. She heard the slam of the car door, then his footsteps returning. He came in carrying a bunch of big, pale yellow chrysanthemums that looked rather wilted. They were wrapped in green paper that had on it the name of the main florist in Blanebury.

With a wry smile he held them out to Robina. 'These were the idea,' he said. 'I went back to Blanebury and bought them. And the rest of the idea was that I should come home, shift Martha out at any cost, and then that you and I should have the place to ourselves, get this room straight, add the finishing touch of these flowers, and then —well, it didn't work out, and I forgot about the flowers and left them in the back of the car, and now, of course, they're no damn good for anything.'

For a moment Robina felt as if the tragedy of Douglas Birch was as nothing compared with the tragedy of the evening that might have been. She touched the wilting petals.

'I think they'd recover in water,' she said. 'Water and aspirins.'

'For God's sake, throw them out!' Sam said. He started walking up and down the room again. 'I know I've been a perfect fool over everything, Robina. But the way I saw it first, when I went into that room and found Douglas, was that a trap had been set for me—set by Martha—and that until I'd seen some flaw in the trap, some mistake that she'd made, I'd just as soon that nobody should know I'd been there. I knew that Denis would back me up for the time being if I asked him to say that I'd been in the lab, and I thought that would give me a little time. I didn't know that anyone had seen me come out of the house.'

'Denis was here a little while ago,' Robina said. 'He said he would back you up, but he said he thought you were making a mistake. He didn't know you hadn't told me about having been to the house.'

'I didn't know Denis had been here.'

'Yes, he arrived just as Ringrose was leaving. And he told Ringrose that you'd been in the lab, and Ringrose told him flatly that he was lying and that as we'd got it all fixed up between us he was going straight to the police with the information that he'd seen you leaving the house.' She was still holding the flowers, unwinding the green paper and then the raffia that tied the stalks together. 'Sam, hadn't you better go to the police yourself now—as soon as possible?'

'It looks like it.' He reached out and took the flowers from her. 'Don't bother with these. They were an idea that misfired. I'll get some others—when all this is over. These can go in the dustbin.' He went out again, taking them with him.

Robina was not sure if he meant to come back or if he had made up his mind to go straight to the police. For a little while she waited, then went out herself, to find that Sam and the car had gone.

Slowly she went back into the house. She wished that he had not gone like that, though she understood why he had done it. All at once she felt completely exhausted and yet assailed by a restlessness that was like an ache all over her body. She wanted neither to work any more nor to sit still, and certainly neither to think nor to feel.

She was full of fears, now that she was alone, fears of the police, of Ringrose, of her own confused thoughts. All through her talk with Sam there had been a thought that she had been keeping at bay, refusing to dwell on it, refusing to speak of it to him. It was the thought that the police, if they convinced themselves that the murder had probably happened at a time when Sam had been in the house, would also be convinced that they knew his motive for murdering Douglas. For if Martha, to satisfy her vanity, or cruelty, or for the sake of some even less comprehensible satisfaction, had made her husband believe that he had reason to be jealous of Sam it seemed unlikely that she would have hesitated to spread the same idea among other people.

Listlessly Robina wound up the cord of the vacuum cleaner and put it away. She emptied the ash trays, swept up the hearth and took the coffee cups out to the kitchen. The game of beggar-my-neighbour had come to an end. The children were out in the garden again, while Mrs Booker, seated at the table, was polishing silver.

Robina told her that she wanted to go into the village to buy one or two things and asked her if she would mind staying till she came back. Really she wanted only to get out of the house for a little while, to see if she could walk off the unpleasant ache of anxiety.

Mrs Booker replied that she could stay until five o'clock. Robina put on her coat, took a shopping basket and went out.

At the village shop she bought oranges, toothpaste and a tin of salmon. Then it occurred to her suddenly to call on the Ringroses.

Her anger against them mounted in her as she walked up the path to the red brick bungalow. It was in her face and in the erectness of her head and her swift speech as Mrs

Ringrose, wearing her spectacles and the same overall and bedroom slippers as the evening before, answered the door.

'I want to speak to your husband,' Robina said.

'He isn't here,' Mrs Ringrose said. Her soft, plump cheeks were pale and her eyes seemed frightened. She started to close the door immediately.

Robina thrust at it with her hand. 'Then I'll speak to you,' she said.

'But I'm very busy just now, I'm ever so sorry.' Mrs Ringrose spoke in a quiet, uncertain way, but she planted her large, soft body against the door. 'I really can't . . .'

'So you know why I want to speak to you,' Robina said.

'I'm sure I don't know what you mean, it's just that I'm busy. Another time I'll be very pleased . . .' She left all her sentences hanging and kept glancing over Robina's shoulder, as if she hoped that help would arrive.

'We'll talk now,' Robina said, 'about the five hundred pounds that your husband took from Douglas Birch yesterday. Was it before or after he was murdered?'

Terror flared in the vague eyes behind the spectacles. Robina thought that the door was going to be slammed in her face. Instead Mrs Ringrose suddenly turned away, leaving the door standing open. Robina went in, closed the door and followed Mrs Ringrose quickly into the sitting-room.

She found her standing with her back to her, with both hands to her head. She seemed to be trying to say something, but the words were strangled by sobs. Her body shook with them. At last Robina managed to make out what she was saying.

'It's his nature! There's nothing I can do about it—it's his nature!'

CHAPTER 13

Robina was caught by surprise. She had never dreamt that she would hear such an admission. She felt that she must have misheard the words. Her anger drained away and she found herself looking at the other woman with shocked sympathy and not knowing what to say next.

Mrs Ringrose had taken off her spectacles and started to dab at her eyes with a handkerchief. 'It's the way he's made,' she said. 'He's always been like that. He doesn't see anything wrong in it. And it's because he loves me, that's what he tells me. He'd never do it just for himself. And he does love me, you see.' She turned and gave Robina a look out of tear-reddened eyes that seemed to challenge her to question this statement.

Robina sat down on the arm of a chair. She could think now of half a dozen different things to say, but she restrained herself from saying any of them. She had a feeling that Mrs Ringrose had a tremendous need to confide in someone, but that an injudicious phrase might make her pull herself together before she had said enough to be useful.

Mrs Ringrose repeated, 'It's because he loves me.' She choked on the last word and the tears streamed again. 'I've told him again and again I don't mind doing without, but it's his pride, you see. It isn't because he's bad, it's just his pride. He can't understand I'd love him just the same without his giving me things. I don't ask for things, really I don't. But it's his pride that he can give me anything a woman could wish for—that's what he says, "Anything a woman could wish for!" And I tell him all I wish for is to live quietly and not worry and go out just once in a while, but he doesn't understand that. That wouldn't satisfy his pride.'

'I see,' Robina said, 'I think I see.'

'He's a good man really—really he's ever so good,' Mrs Ringrose went on. 'He's ever so kind. You should see the way he looks after me when I'm ill. And he's the kindest man alive to children and animals. But he's intolerant, I will say that, he doesn't make allowances for people. "I couldn't take a penny off them if they hadn't done something to be ashamed of," he says. "You don't have to worry, I'm only doing the same as the law would do if it could catch them," he says. "And isn't it right that they should pay?" he says. "You've got to pay for what you do in this world, that's only right. You shouldn't get off scot free with an easy conscience when you've done wrong." I tell him nobody's perfect and you've got to make allowances, and that it's not for him to judge. But that's where his pride comes in, you see. He doesn't realize he can do wrong himself. That's his nature—there's nothing I can do about it—that's just his nature!'

'And the five hundred pounds?' Robina said.

Mrs Ringrose lowered the handkerchief with which she had kept dabbing at her eyes. 'I don't know anything about five hundred pounds,' she said.

'Five hundred pounds he took from Mr Birch yesterday.'

'Oh, he never did!' The look of panic was there again. 'Never!'

'I thought that was what we were talking about,' Robina said.

'Never! He'd have told me if—if anything like that had happened. He always tells me everything. He told me about going to see you and telling you about your husband and I thought that was why you came to see me. And I knew how you must be feeling, because I know how it feels when you love your husband, and I was really angry with him about that, I really was, but he never went near Mr Birch yesterday, never!' The hurrying sentences drowned once more in tears.

118

'But he got money from Mr Birch in the past, didn't he?'
Robina was surprised at the sound of detachment in her
own voice.

'But he didn't know he was doing wrong, he never thought
of doing wrong,' Mrs Ringrose said. 'Don't you understand?
It's as if he feels he's got a right to it—don't you understand
that? You ought to try and understand.' The sobbing voice
had an undertone of anger.

'I think,' Robina said slowly and distinctly, 'that he got
five hundred pounds from Mr Birch yesterday.'

'And didn't tell me? You don't know him. He tells me
everything. If he'd been there, if he'd done that murder—
which is what you're trying to make me think, because
you're afraid of what your own husband may have done, I
know that—he'd have told me. He knows I'd love him
whatever he did and he trusts me. So I know he never went
there. Besides, he's the kindest man alive and he'd never
have touched a hair of Mr Birch's head. You ask your own
husband what he was doing yesterday and what he did with
the money, if there's money missing, and don't come trying
to frighten me about poor Harold. He's a good man, you've
got to understand that.'

Robina stood up. 'Perhaps I understand poor Harold, but
I don't understand you.'

'I love him, that's all,' Mrs Ringrose said. 'I'd love him
whatever he did. But I know he isn't a murderer.'

'I could understand your loving him if he was a murderer,'
Robina said, 'but a blackmailer . . .'

As she let herself out of the house she heard Mrs Ringrose
sobbing again, 'It's his nature, it isn't his fault, he can't
help it.'

Robina walked quickly down the path to the road. An
intense revulsion, which she had been trying to control while
she was in the bungalow, overcame her so sharply as she
hurried away that she felt she might actually be sick.

What was this love, she wondered, to which the woman

119

was clinging, a love that destroyed her own pride and strangled her conscience? What did it mean to be in the grip of such a love? To Robina it seemed just then that there was something obscene about it, as ugly in its way as the crime it tolerated.

Yet loyalty was a virtue. The love that forgave all things tended to be highly regarded. Was her own sense of disgust, then, the sign of a cold heart, or of a lack of imagination encouraged by a too fortunate experience of other people? How would she behave herself if she discovered that her heart was in the keeping of someone evil or contemptible?

As the question came into her mind, something that felt like a few pricking drops of cold water tingled along her spine. It was a horrible moment and the after-effect of it was an intense self-disgust. She walked even faster than before, as if that might help her to forget what had happened in her when she asked herself that unnecessary question.

Reaching home and letting herself in, she realized at once that other questions were being asked there. Questioning, it seemed, was in the air. Closing the door, she heard it clearly.

'Have you ever seen a whale?'

The questioner was Miles. Hearing the quiet, deep voice that answered him, Robina knew that his victim was Pete Hillman.

'No,' Pete said. 'I wish I had.'

'But you know about whales?' Miles said as Robina came into the room.

'Sure,' Pete answered, starting to get to his feet.

But Miles, who had been leaning against his knee, did his best to prevent this. 'How come?' he asked.

Pete grinned at Robina. 'We've been through it once already with sharks,' he said. 'I guess he's kind of checking up.'

'Don't let me interrupt,' Robina said, putting down her shopping-basket and taking off her coat.

'Well, let's see,' Pete said, turning his attention back to Miles. 'How do I know about whales? I guess I've read about them, and seen pictures of them, and talked to people who have seen them.'

'Have you ever seen a walrus?' Miles asked.

'No,' Pete said.

'But you know about walruses?'

'Sure.'

'How come?'

'Well, I guess I've read about them and seen pictures of them, and talked to people who have seen them . . . What's he after, Robina? A theory of knowledge?'

'I wouldn't put it past him,' she said. 'Have you seen Sam, Pete?'

'No, but I heard he'd been looking for me and I wanted to see him too. There's a question I want to ask him.'

'Questions!' Robina said. 'I've just been asking some, but I didn't get much out of it . . . No, Miles!' She had seen him about to continue his catechism. 'That's enough questions from you. It's Pete's turn now. Run along and find Miranda.'

Reluctantly, but with his usual good temper, Miles went out and Robina dropped into a chair opposite Pete.

'I can tell you why Sam was looking for you,' she said. 'It's something about some ice in a drink.'

'And I thought it was sure to be about this murder.'

'So it is,' she said.

He gave her a reflective look. 'Have you ever seen a murderer? . . . No. But you know about murderers? . . . Sure. How come? . . . You know, that boy's got something. How do any of us know about murderers? How would you know one if you saw one?' His tone disturbed her.

'The fact is, I shouldn't, Pete,' she said. 'How would you?'

'I guess I've read about them, and seen pictures of them, and maybe I've talked to people who have seen them, though

I'm not sure about that. But the truth is, I shouldn't know any more than you, and that goes for the rest of us. And that's on all our minds, not only wondering if we're looking at a murderer but wondering if we look like a murderer to the other guy . . . What's this about the ice, Robina?'

'You don't look like a murderer to us, Pete, if that's what you're getting at,' she said.

'Maybe I don't to you, but I'm not quite so sure about Sam. Particularly if he wants to ask me about something like ice. It's those little questions about those little things that mean trouble. Tell me about the ice.'

'It's the ice and one or two other things,' she said, 'that make him think you were in that house sometime yesterday. And because the police probably have to be told about the ice, he wanted to ask you first if you were.'

'I was,' he said. 'I went there with him, remember?'

'Of course!' she exclaimed. 'And you were there on your own, weren't you, waiting for the police while Sam came over here? Whyever didn't we think of that? Of course that explains it.'

'I don't see how it can explain anything about ice,' he said. 'I didn't help myself to a drink while I was waiting, if that's what you mean.'

She was disappointed. 'You're sure you didn't?'

'Quite sure.'

'That's a pity. It would have explained everything. You see, Pete, what happened was this. Miss Woods says that before she went out for the afternoon she filled the ice trays in the fridge and put out two clean glass cloths in the kitchen, and later that evening she found that some of the ice cubes were gone and that one of the glass cloths had been used. And she told all this to Mrs Booker and asked her to ask Sam to advise her on whether or not she ought to tell this to the police. It's such a small thing in itself, and yet she felt that it needed explaining—as it probably does, don't you think?'

'Sure,' Pete said. 'And I can see how Sam's explained it.'

'But he hasn't said anything about it to anyone yet.'

'Explained it to himself, then.'

She moved her hands in a conciliatory gesture. 'Don't be angry, Pete—please. Sam's in an awful mess himself.' She would have liked to tell him all about the mess. It seemed only fair, in view of what she had been asking him. But at the same time it seemed impossible to do so without Sam's knowledge. She compromised by telling him a little. 'He was in that house himself at one time in the afternoon and there are going to be people who believe he had a motive.'

He looked at her steadily for a moment. 'But you aren't one of them.' He smiled. 'I'm not angry. A little nervous, maybe, but I was that before I came here. And I knew Sam had been to the house sometime yesterday or guessed it was likely, and I didn't think he knew about the little piece of evidence that suggested it. But the police know.'

'They know already?' Robina said sharply.

'They know this one thing. You know Douglas was reading when he was killed?'

'I know that's how it looked.'

'D'you know what he was reading?'

'No.'

'Does Sam?'

'He hasn't said anything about it.'

'The book was half under the body and I know Sam didn't touch it while I was there. But I took a look at it after he'd gone. I don't know why I did—just a kind of curiosity, I guess. And the book was Sam's copy of *The Kinetics of Enzyme Action*, by Carradoc and Peabody. It's got his name in it. And I know it couldn't have been in the house earlier than yesterday, because he loaned it to me a few weeks ago and I returned it on Wednesday morning, when I met him just as he was starting out for London. He must have thrown it in the back of the car, because it was still there in the evening, when he picked up Edna, Iris and me on the way back from the station. I know, because I sat on it.' His eyes were anxious. 'The police didn't tell him, did they?'

'No,' Robina said.

'I've been asking myself ever since if I shouldn't have gotten rid of that book while I had the chance,' Pete went on. 'I could have gotten rid of it and put something else there instead. At the time I guess I was too scared to think of it. And that brings me back to the other things I've been scared of, the thing I wanted to talk over with you and Sam.'

'The ice,' Robina said.

'For God's sake!' he said. 'I don't know anything about any ice. Am I really the only guy here who takes ice in a drink?'

She laughed. 'It looks as if there must be someone else, doesn't it?'

'Only you don't think there is. I get it. But I can't help you there. I really don't know anything about it. I wasn't in that house yesterday until I went there with Sam. But I *was* going there when I met Sam in the village and stopped him and suggested we have a drink. And if Miss Woods hadn't come running in here screaming murder, almost the minute I arrived here with Sam, I'd have left and I'd have gone back to that house to see Douglas. He was expecting me sometime that evening.' He made a reasonless, jerky movement with one hand, which told Robina that he was tenser than he appeared. 'I was going to collect five hundred pounds,' he said.

She looked at him incredulously. '*You* were?'

'Oh yes—Pete the blackmailer.' He grinned. But that betraying hand was now tugging at a loose thread in the worn chair cover. 'No, it wasn't blackmail. It was an idea I had of helping the guy—maybe not a very good idea, but still that's what it was. When he asked me if I could help him I said, "Why not?" But it *was* illegal. And I'd just as soon not have to tell the cops about it.'

'But what were you going to do for him with five hundred

pounds? . . . Oh!' She had suddenly understood. 'Dollars!'

'That's right,' Pete said. 'He was crazy to go to the United States and stay there for some months, but when he applied for dollars your Treasury would only let him have enough for a few weeks. So he suggested to me he should loan me five hundred pounds to live on here and I could arrange to pay him back over there. So that's how it was. I arranged with my folks to pay him the dollars when he got there, and I was going to see him yesterday to collect the pounds. A purely private arrangement—all the same, to the best of my knowledge and belief, it was illegal. And it was some other guy who collected the pounds, and that makes it kind of awkward for me, because I'm not sure how I'm going to prove that, all the more so if some secret ice eater called on Douglas yesterday, and everyone's going to think it must have been me. Well, what do you think about it?' His tone as he finished was flippant but Robina could see that he was deeply uneasy.

'So that's why you jumped to the conclusion straight away that there'd been a robbery,' she said. 'That worried Sam.'

'I could see it did.'

'Tell me,' she said, 'who else knew of this arrangement —apart from your family in America?'

'Only Martha. She was mad at me too. She tried a little fast work on me to stop things. Very gratifying—until I realized what it was all about.'

'Did you know that Douglas wanted to take Martha with him?'

'Sure. That's why I decided to help. I figured he could use a little help in that direction.'

A number of Robina's ideas were undergoing rapid readjustment. She tried to visualize the little scene, the meeting between Pete and Martha, and to recall what the quality in it had been that had made both Sam and herself leap to the conclusion that Pete was the man with whom Martha was in love, for whom she wanted Douglas to divorce her.

He was going on. 'The way I worked it out, what those two needed most was to make up their minds what they wanted. If Douglas went to the United States, either Martha would go with him or she wouldn't. If she did, that would be fine. Maybe they'd have a good time together and come home liking each other a little. If she wouldn't, maybe that would convince Douglas to let her go, then what he'd need himself would be a change of scene. There's nothing like a change of scene to mend a broken heart, or so they tell me. But you still haven't told me, Robina, how much of this do I need to tell the cops?'

She leant her head on her hands, trying to think clearly. 'I can't see at the moment why you need tell them any of it,' she said, 'but that will depend, I suppose, on where that money turns up—if it ever does. I can't see why it should matter for the present if it goes on looking like another blackmail payment. But let's talk that over with Sam when he gets back. He—' She hesitated, looking up at Pete uncertainly. Her small, sharp face was suddenly haggard. 'He went to see the police, to tell them that he was in that house yesterday afternoon, but I thought he'd be back before now. They seem to be keeping him an awfully long time . . .' Her voice faltered.

Pete was out of his chair in an instant and kneeling beside her, taking both her hands in his. 'For heaven's sake!' he said. 'Why didn't you tell me this before? You've had this on your mind all the time I was talking? But listen, you've nothing to worry about. What if he was there? Nobody's going to think Sam's a murderer. They may keep him for hours, questioning him, but that's all that will happen. If there's no evidence it's all that *can* happen.'

'But there is evidence, Pete.' His sympathy had been fatal and her tears were beginning to flow. 'It's false evidence, it has to be, because it's evidence against Sam—but how can the police be expected to know that? If you'd never seen a whale, how would you know one when you met one except

126

by evidence?' She tried to laugh at her own attempt at a joke, but failed, and the tears flowed faster.

'You've got to remember, that inspector's probably seen plenty of whales—and sharks, not to mention sea serpents,' Pete said. 'It's people like you and me who couldn't pass marine biology. He looked to me like an intelligent sort of guy. You've got nothing to worry about. I'm sure you've got nothing to worry about. Now what'll cheer you up? A drink?'

She shook her head dumbly.

'Then how about a nice cosy chat about your allergies—that does people a lot of good.'

'I haven't any,' she sobbed.

'I was afraid not. You just haven't caught on here yet what useful things they are. There's nothing like a good allergy for propping up the ego.' He looked at her helplessly. 'Robina, sweetheart—'

He broke off as quick footsteps sounded in the passage. The door opened and Iris Swinson came in. She stood still in the doorway, staring.

Pete sprang to his feet. His face was scarlet. 'Hold it, Robina—don't say anything!' he said violently. 'You just don't know what this girl's capable of thinking when she puts her mind to it!'

CHAPTER 14

Iris's face was as red as Pete's. She looked shy and miserable and extremely young, but as if she believed that by standing there in a firmly planted, rather aggressive way she could conceal these things about herself.

'I didn't know you were here,' she said to Pete. 'If I had I shouldn't have come.'

'So now you hate me,' he said. 'Now you can't stand the

sight of me.' He was looking at her warily, as if she might explode in his face. Robina had never seen his poise so upset. 'So what am I supposed to do about it? Get out fast?'

'You got out fast this morning,' Iris said. 'You didn't even have breakfast. That was a ridiculous thing to do.'

'Believe me, it was the only thing to do.'

'But without breakfast!'

'A man can go without food for much longer than you think,' he said.

'But it was such a ludicrously *melodramatic* thing to do.'

'Who's talking about melodrama? Who started the melodrama last night? And all because—because—'

A faint sparkle came into Iris's eyes, as if there was something that she enjoyed in the memory of the scene she had made the evening before. 'I'm never melodramatic at breakfast,' she said. 'It isn't the right time for it.'

'There's no right time for it.'

'Oh, there is.' She smiled. The discovery that she had caught him off balance was rapidly restoring Iris's shattered self-confidence. 'It can feel quite wonderful sometimes to make an abject fool of oneself. I did make a fool of myself, of course. But I'll probably go on doing it as long as you go on making love to that murderess. It's for your own sake entirely. After all, you are a foreigner, and there are lots of things about us here that you don't understand, and so we have a sort of responsibility to see that you don't get into trouble.'

'Trouble! How do you like that?' Pete said shrilly. 'First of all, Martha is not a murderess. Secondly, I have not been making love to her. Thirdly, you're the one who'll need to be kept out of trouble if you go around saying things like that.'

Robina, whose tears had stopped and who had quite recovered herself, looked from one face to the other, saw the fierce concentration on each other revealed by both faces, and wondered how she and Sam could have been so mistaken about the meaning of the scene the evening before between Pete and Martha.

But Edna also had been mistaken, when she had said that Pete did not know that Iris was walking the earth. He was intensely aware of her, though in a slightly bewildered way, as if he did not quite know how this had come about.

Perhaps, Robina thought, it was missing his breakfast that had brought it about. There was nothing like fasting for clearing the mind. Perhaps Iris's melodrama, her explosion of unexpected jealousy, had opened his eyes to more than the state of her emotions. At all events, his embarrassment and defensiveness were too blatant to be real and almost certainly he was enjoying himself.

Robina was also inclined to think that Iris had sensed this, even if she was not quite sure of it. The flush that had covered her face and neck had faded, leaving only a slightly brighter colour than usual in her cheeks, and there was no trace left of the shamefaced and sullen manner in which she had greeted Pete when she first came into the room.

'Well, I don't know what you call making love,' Iris said, 'if that wasn't it.'

'Far from it,' Pete answered. 'It was a simple and natural response to Martha's particular type of personality.'

'But she's a murderess, Pete! You must take a little care about the people you get simple and natural with.'

This, Robina thought, was where she got up, made some appropriate excuse and went out of the room, and she had started to do this when she heard Mrs Booker's heavy tread in the hall. The door opened.

Mrs Booker was in her overcoat, with the usual scarf tied over her head. 'I really ought to go now, Mrs Mellows,' she said hesitantly. 'There's some things I ought to see to at home.'

'Of course, Mrs Booker.' Robina went to the door to meet her. 'It was awfully good of you to stay. It's been a tremendous help.'

'You'll soon be straight now,' Mrs Booker said. 'I'll come in again tomorrow, if you like. I can always take the children off your hands for a while, if you've nothing much else for me to do. You'll soon be straight. It's a nice house and when you're straight you'll be very happy here. I'll come tomorrow.' She turned away. But before closing the door, she turned back again to Robina. 'About Miss Woods,' she said. 'What ought I to tell her?'

'About the ice, you mean,' Robina said. 'We talked it over, but I'm not sure—'

Pete interrupted. 'Tell her to tell the police about it, Robina.'

She gave him a direct, questioning look. He returned it, nodding his head.

'Well then,' Robina said, 'that's what I'd advise her to do, Mrs Booker. Tell the police about the ice and the tea cloth.'

'It seems such a small thing to mention,' Mrs Booker said uncertainly.

With a good deal of agitation Iris asked, 'What's this about ice?'

'You tell her,' Robina said to Pete. 'I want to have a word with Mrs Booker.'

She went out with her, pulling the door of the sitting-room shut behind her.

Robina knew what she wanted to say to Mrs Booker, but she was nervous of saying it and not sure how to set about it. Going to the front door, she went out into the garden with her. She was surprised for a moment at how warm it felt out of doors. The sky was covered with low cloud and the air felt moist against her face.

'I should think it's going to rain soon,' she said.

'That's right,' Mrs Booker answered. 'I'm glad I did my washing early this week. Monday was a wonderful day for hanging it out. I had it all dry by dinnertime.'

'I want to thank you, Mrs Booker,' Robina went on, 'for helping us today . . .' She hesitated.

'That's all right,' Mrs Booker said. 'I could see you'd want a hand with the children, things happening like they have. You don't want them puzzling their heads about what's going on. And I don't mind doing a long day, if I can just get off my feet. It's the standing does it to me, if I don't take care. But it's generally all right so long as I take a pinch of mustard in a cup of coffee with my supper every night. I've wonderful health really. I never was really ill but once and that came of eating an unripe pear. It stuck on my chest, you see. It stuck on my chest for six weeks. The pain was terrible and afterwards I was weak as a kitten. I took herb tea for that, with just two teaspoons of rum in it —that put me right in the end and it's the only time I ever been what you might call ill.'

'Mrs Booker, there's something else I wanted to say,' Robina said. 'It's about your husband. I hope you don't mind my speaking of him.'

'I don't mind, my dear,' Mrs Booker said. 'I like to speak of him. I miss him much more if I don't speak of him. I was always laughing at the little fellow and even now it suddenly comes over me and I start laughing . . . He was very religious—it come on him suddenly when he was past sixty —and sometimes I'd have to go and hide myself in the scullery so he shouldn't hear me laughing when he was kneeling down by his bed in his nightshirt with his little legs sticking out and his face so serious. I try to be a Christian and I've been to church regular all my life, but he got it sudden like, and I reckon that's why he was so serious. Really, I couldn't help laughing. But he never minded.'

This seemed only to make it harder to say what Robina had in mind. 'It's about Mr Ovenden,' she said.

She saw the life die out of the old face. Mrs Booker's eyes became anxious and evasive.

Robina hurried on. 'I think a great many people believe he killed your husband. My husband, who knows him very well, never believed it. And now Mrs Birch has told Mrs

Swinson that she's known all this time that it was Mr Birch who killed him. I wanted you to know because—well, because I think Mr Ovenden has suffered a great deal, knowing what people thought.'

Mrs Booker was silent. The anxious look deepened. Her hands began to twist the handles of the cretonne bag she carried. At last she said, 'I tried to forgive him. I prayed to be able to forgive him. I thought, "He's got a terrible load to carry all his life, it isn't for me to make it heavier," but when I saw him face to face it was as much as I could do . . .' She drew a deep breath. 'Poor young fellow. Thank God I didn't say anything. But the other one and her—they let him suffer like that?'

'She was protecting her husband,' Robina said. 'Perhaps one can't altogether blame her.'

'If so, it's one of the only things she's ever done for him,' Mrs Booker said. 'But I'm glad you told me, Mrs Mellows. Poor young fellow. I'm sorry I was doing an injustice to him, in my thoughts, but at least I didn't say anything. I thought, "You can do a bad thing in a moment and spend the rest of your life repenting of it, and no one can tell what sorrow there is in your heart," so I didn't say anything. Well, I'm glad. But for them to have let him suffer like that . . .' She gave a puzzled shake of her head. 'I'll be back in the morning,' she added and tramped off.

Robina went back into the house. She went to the kitchen, where she found Miranda and Miles, both crouching on the floor, collaborating in drawing a small picture with coloured chalks. The picture was mainly Miranda's creation, and was of the house that all children draw, a square box with two windows upstairs, two downstairs, a door between them and a chimney at the top, with smoke coming out of it. There were some red, daisylike flowers in a row in front of the house, and Miles, whose interests were mainly zoological, was adding some fauna to the garden. But since Miranda, contemptuous of his abilities, had allowed him space only on the outer edges of her picture, his creatures, not particularly recognizable as mammal, bird or fish, seemed to float around the house, rather like cherubs or little dragons, giving the picture an interestingly mediaeval air.

'We're doing this for Mrs Booker,' Miranda said. 'We think she's nice.'

'We'll do one for you too,' Miles promised Robina, perhaps more aware than Miranda of the possibilities of feminine jealousy.

'That'll be lovely,' Robina said, 'but perhaps you could do it tomorrow. I'm going to get your tea now, then you can have your baths and go to bed.'

'We can't go to bed till we've finished this picture,' Miranda said. 'We promised Mrs Booker.'

Robina agreed to that and set about getting their tea. Presently she heard the door of the sitting-room open, then low voices in the hall, then the sound of the front door opening and closing. Immediately afterwards Iris came out to the kitchen.

She looked as if she were about to plunge into speech but, seeing the children, stopped. Miranda showed her the picture and Iris praised its beauty, but her thoughts were certainly not on what she was saying. Her movements were restless and her eyes brilliant in their concentration on some inner vision.

'What happened to Pete?' Robina asked.

'He's gone. He—' Iris stopped again and laughed nervously. 'He said he was going to tell the police about the money. Isn't he a fool?'

'You're sure he didn't run away from you again?' Robina asked, busily cutting bread and butter.

'Yes—no. I mean, it was quite different from last night. I was *awful* last night, Robina, I'm utterly ashamed, only I know I'd do it again. They made me *mad*.' Iris's quick speech, her way of emphasizing odd words, was even more marked than usual. 'She came in—Martha, I mean—and went straight into Pete's arms, and he—you know what he's like—he started clucking over her like a mother hen. I felt so *furious* I just said—well, everything! Then I cried about it half the night. I've never felt so awful. I wanted to die. But seeing that woman who'd just killed her husband trying to take hold of Pete, I couldn't stop myself. And I didn't mean to say anything about myself and I'm not sure that I did, but I suppose I gave myself away hopelessly. Now I don't mind that, in fact, I rather like the feeling, and Pete . . .' She started to smile, then seemed to forget that she had been in the middle of saying something and, dropping onto one of the straight-backed kitchen chairs, sat gazing raptly before her, leaving that half-smile on her face, as it were, to take care of itself.

Robina glanced at the children and saw that their heads were close together a few inches from the floor. She trusted that they were too engrossed in their picture to be listening. 'And I thought it was Denis you were in love with,' she said.

A faint frown replaced Iris's smile, but the lost, dreaming look did not quite fade from her eyes. 'That's what Pete said. He said he'd always taken it for granted. But I was never in love with Denis at all. He just held onto me as if he needed me, somehow, and I never knew what to do about it. He wasn't in love with me but he wanted to be with me. I think, you know, he hasn't any real interest in women. He thinks about hardly anything but his work. If he ever gets married it'll probably be with a woman about fifteen years older than himself, who'll mother him and look after him. I told him all that once.' She gave a sharp sigh. She had come out of her dream and there was worry in her eyes. 'That was on the day of the Birches' New Year party. Denis and I had a sort of quarrel in the afternoon. He'd been getting awfully difficult in a queer sort of way and it was getting on my nerves. You can understand that, can't you?'

Robina nodded.

'Well, I suppose I said something that hurt him and he flew into a fearful rage,' Iris went on. 'Just occasionally he does. His temper's perfectly frightful when he loses it. I mean, he doesn't just say a few nasty things and go out and slam the door. He goes dead white and trembles all over and says nothing at all and you feel that what he wants is to get his hands on your throat. That was the first time I'd ever seen it happen and I was scared. I mean, really scared. And I said I wouldn't go to the party. Afterwards I wished I'd gone, because if I had, things mightn't have happened as they did . . . That's to say, as we all thought they did.'

'You mean you believed it was Denis who'd killed Booker,' Robina said.

Iris looked confused. 'I never made up my mind. Mother said he hadn't, and so did Sam, but I—I suppose I did think it was Denis. And I blamed myself mostly, because perhaps if I'd understood him a bit better none of it would have happened. Only now we know it wasn't Denis.'

'I wonder,' Robina said thoughtfully, 'I wonder if you weren't a little in love with Denis, and it was only after the accident that you decided you weren't.'

Iris flushed suddenly and deeply. 'Oh, I don't know,' she said. 'It doesn't matter, does it?'

'I don't suppose so.'

'You know, he isn't really quite human. He's a dear, I'm very fond of him, but he isn't human. Some women seem to be awfully attracted to him just because of it, they do really, isn't that queer? But I think that even if you're tremendously intelligent you ought to be human.'

'Well, no one could dream of saying that Pete wasn't human.'

'He's a lot *too* human,' Iris said swiftly. 'I mean, it's all very well enjoying it when a good-looking woman throws herself at you, but when she happens to be a murderess . . .'

The look of confusion returned. 'Only, if it's true about the ice, she can't be a murderess, can she?'

'That's going a little fast for me,' Robina said. 'What's the connection?'

'Well, if somebody wanted to frame Pete by making it look as if he'd been at the house in the afternoon—and that's what the ice being missing suggests, isn't it?—then that wouldn't be Martha, would it?'

'You mean because she's in love with him?'

'Of course.'

'I think you're making two guesses there that aren't quite justified,' Robina said. 'It's only a guess that the ice was removed for that reason, and personally I think it's a far too subtle reason to be real. After all, the murderer couldn't even be sure that anyone would notice that the ice cubes had gone. And the other guess is that Martha's in love with Pete.'

'If she isn't, she wants us to think that she is,' Iris said.

Robina went to the refrigerator for a bottle of milk. 'She wants us to think . . . ? You know, there could be something in that.'

'But who would have taken the ice?'

'I haven't the slightest idea.'

'I didn't take any ice,' Miles said, looking up with a deliberately sweet smile of conscious rectitude.

Iris gave a laugh. She stood up. 'I'm sorry—I oughtn't to have started talking about these things. I think I'd better go home now. I've got some apologizing to do all round.'

'I like ice,' Miles went on, anxious not to be misunderstood. 'But I didn't take any.'

'I wonder what he did take,' Robina said, smiling. She followed Iris into the hall. 'Will the apologies include Martha?'

A gleam came into Iris's eyes. 'That'll depend on how she acts up with Pete . . . You know, Robina, I don't think he hates me as much as I thought he would.'

Robina ventured no answer to this and after a moment Iris herself decided to laugh at it.

When she had gone Robina returned to the kitchen to give the children their tea and to try to talk to them for a while in the way that they expected. It was not easy. All the time she was listening for the sound of Sam's key in the lock, again and again imagining that she heard it and convincing herself that every car that passed was stopping at the gate.

She had not realized before how many cars went by at this time of the evening, or how many sounds, perhaps the tapping of a twig against a window pane, or the rattle of a pebble in the road, under the foot of a passer-by, could sound like the click of a latch. The children were impatient too for Sam's return, vaguely disturbed because they had seen so little of him all day and because of all the unusual coming and going in the house. On the whole they were prepared to accept this as a part of the adventure of a move, but Miranda particularly was a little suspicious that there was more to it than this and that something was going on around her that she was not supposed to notice. Soon, Robina thought, this was going to mean trouble.

When the children were in bed she read to them for a while, and it was while she was doing this that she at last heard Sam come in.

Miles and Miranda heard it too and shouted for him to come up to say good night to them. He came upstairs. When he came into the room he was smiling, but Robina thought at once that she had never before seen him look so tired. Lines that she had never noticed before seemed to be etched as deeply into his pale face as if they had been there for years and there was something slack and devitalized about his whole body.

He gave one swift glance at Robina, but after that would not meet her eyes, as if he feared that in doing so he might too easily betray too much of his feelings in front of the children.

Miranda, sensing that there was something unusual in the air and thinking that advantage might somehow be taken of it, demanded that he should not merely say good night but should stay and read to them. Robina thought that, with that dull, exhausted look in his eyes and the slight nervous puckering of the eyelids round them, he was certain to refuse. But he not only agreed, sitting down on the edge of Miranda's bed and taking the book from Robina, but when he had been reading for a little while did not seem to want to stop. It was only when both heads had sunk back on the pillows and eyes were drowsily closing that he shut the book and went softly out of the room.

In a curious way the little scene had deeply alarmed Robina. It seemed to her that Sam was not only trying to avoid talking to her but at the same time was trying to clutch at something and hold onto it fast, as if he felt it slipping out of his grasp.

Downstairs she drew the curtains, lit the fire and poured out drinks. Sam took his and drank it quickly. She saw him shudder slightly as its strength went through him. Pouring himself another, he settled into a chair, stretched his legs across the hearthrug and looked up at her with the same lifeless smile that had disturbed her upstairs.

'Sorry I took so long,' he said.

'What happened?'

'Awfully little. Nothing, really.'

'Then why were you so long?'

'I wanted to see that man Morton. He wasn't there, so I went away again.'

'You mean you haven't been to the police at all?'

'Oh yes, I went back later. I saw him then and told him that I'd lied to him before about not having seen Douglas yesterday. He didn't try to make it easy for me. One can't blame him, I suppose. I kept trying to remind myself that I didn't blame him, but it didn't work. I spent an hour hating the ground he walked on, the chair he was sitting on, the air he was breathing. And even now I can't stop, though he was only doing his job and not being too bad about it. God, hatred wears one out!'

'Some people seem able to live on it,' Robina said. She sat down on the hearthrug. 'Like Ringrose. Did you tell him about Ringrose?'

'Yes. But there was something queer about that. Ringrose hadn't been to see him, or so Morton said. He hadn't told the police anything about having seen me come out of the Birches' house. Yet Morton seemed to know that I'd been there. He told me he'd been waiting for me to change my story.'

'I think I can explain that,' Robina said. 'You left a book in the house. Pete was here this afternoon and he told me about it. It's a book by Somebody and Peabody and it's got your name in it. And it's the book that Douglas was reading when he was killed.'

He looked at her incredulously. 'Carradoc and Peabody? *The Kinetics of Enzyme Action*? . . .' Suddenly he laughed. Robina did not understand why, but for the first time since he had come in the deadness went out of his eyes. 'Did you tell Pete about the ice?' he asked.

'Yes, and he still says he never went to the house, but that he was going there when you met him.' She went on to tell him the rest of Pete's story, of his deal with Douglas and the other events of the afternoon.

By the end of it Sam was looking almost his normal self. A third drink helped, and a meal, hurriedly produced by Robina, mostly out of tins, lowered still more the tension of anxiety.

'I'm awfully sorry about the food,' Robina said, 'but I think I'll have things running normally by Monday.'

'Tinned salmon was the passion of my youth,' Sam said. 'It feels quite soothing to revert to it. Robina, d'you know what was really worrying me when I came in?'

'You were scared,' she said.

139

'Oh yes, and I still am. But there was something else. About the police knowing that I'd been to see Douglas, when Ringrose hadn't told them. I didn't know about the book, you see. So I couldn't think how they could have found out unless Denis had told them. I didn't believe it, but I couldn't get the idea out of my mind. I'm not very proud of it.'

'Well, he needn't know.'

'No, all the same I wish it hadn't happened. This feeling I've got that someone's trying to get me into a trap, tangle me up in a lot of false evidence—perhaps I'm exaggerating it all, I don't know, but there it is—it's a feeling that plays hell with one's trust in one's fellow beings.'

She nodded in agreement. But there, mainly out of weariness, they left the matter. Tentatively at first, as if there were something almost improper about it, they began to talk of other things.

Robina slept soundly that night, dreamlessly, with one arm curved under her head, scarcely moving. It was one of the nights in which consciousness was so completely blotted out that it seemed to form a gulf between one day and the next, making it harder than usual to pick up the threads of yesterday's living. Waking slowly, with nothing behind her but the darkness of deep sleep, it was the day before that seemed like a dream that she must have had in the night.

But Sam had slept very little. She knew that as soon as she looked at his face. He looked as if he had been lying there merely waiting for her to wake up, and as soon as he saw that her eyes were open he sat up.

'I've something to show you,' he said. 'I couldn't sleep much, so I went downstairs to make myself some tea, and in the kitchen I found this.'

He held out to her the picture that had been drawn for Mrs Booker by Miles and Miranda.

Robina looked at it stupidly, she felt that she could not

be awake. Sam's tone and the gay little picture together made no sense.

'What's the matter with it?' she asked.

'Turn it over,' he said.

She did so and saw that the piece of paper on which Miles and Miranda had drawn the little house with the red flowers on it and the queer animals suspended in the air all around it was a five-pound note.

CHAPTER 15

Robina sat up beside Sam, rubbing her eyes. The light in the room was dim and she thought at first that it must still be very early, then she realized that the windows were curtained in fog.

'Miles said he hadn't taken any ice,' she said. 'I said I wondered what else he *had* taken, but really I was only joking.'

'The money Douglas got for Pete was in five-pound notes,' Sam said.

The air was cold on Robina's shoulders. They looked at one another in silence.

'We'll have to go about this very carefully,' Sam went on, 'or he'll never tell us where he found it.'

'He probably doesn't know what it is,' Robina said. 'I doubt if he's ever seen a five-pound note before.'

'You'd better do the questioning,' Sam said. 'You'll know how to handle it better than I shall.'

'The main thing is not to let it seem important. But, Sam, where *could* he have found it?'

'Somewhere it was left for him to find.'

She gave a scared look into his eyes.

He said, 'He wouldn't have taken it out of anyone's handbag.'

'No, I don't think so.'

'And he wouldn't shine as a pickpocket.'

'No. But all the same . . .'

'You mean that no one could guess what he'd do with it if he found it.'

'Yes. He might have made it into a boat and sailed it in a puddle. Or he might have torn it into little pieces and strewn them around in the garden. Or he might simply have brought it to us—in which case we might have hidden it or handed it over to the police.'

'According to how honest we were feeling, or how frightened. Yes, I see what you mean. But in that case . . .' He gave a laugh. 'In that case, you know, it looks as if there may be another ninety-nine of these hidden in the house, which weren't meant to be found. And if so, it does away with the last faint hope that Douglas was murdered by a stray burglar who got away with a better haul than he expected, because a stray burglar would hardly hide his loot here.'

'Oh dear, let's stop all this wondering and guessing,' Robina said, putting her hands to her head. 'There's no end to what one can imagine, once one starts. Let's wait till we've talked to Miles, then see what sense we can make of it all.'

Sam threw the bedclothes back and stood up, reaching for his dressing gown. 'I'll go down and make some tea,' he said. 'We may be more lucid after it.'

While he was downstairs making the tea Robina got up and dressed. The feeling that there was trouble ahead, including an interview with the police about the missing money, made her decide against wearing her jeans. She had a moderate liking for her own appearance in jeans, but doubted if anyone else shared it. Choosing a tweed skirt and a brightly coloured woollen blouse, she put her hair up carefully instead of merely tying it back with the rather tattered yellow ribbon, then took some trouble with her make-up.

Sam, coming in in the middle of it with the tea tray, grinned as he met her eyes in the mirror. 'It almost looks as if you consider our situation desperate,' he said.

'Not quite that,' she said, 'but I don't think it'll hurt if I look like a good, brave little woman when we go into action with the police, as I suppose we shall have to. Anyway, I know you prefer it, and besides, the dirty work's mostly done.'

'Of the move, I suppose you mean, not the dirty work at the crossroads.' He put the tray down on a chest of drawers and poured out the tea. 'It'd be nice to think we were near the end of that too, but I doubt it somehow.'

They agreed that they would ask the children no questions about the five-pound note until after breakfast.

When Robina began it, she started by admiring the picture, but was told by Miranda that it was not really much good. Miranda was in one of her superior moods and explained that Miles had spoilt the picture.

'Think of putting a horse in the sky,' she said. 'He's such a silly little boy, he doesn't know better.'

Robina looked at the little green and purple scribble in the top left-hand corner of the picture and wondered how Miranda had managed to identify it as a horse.

'*Is* it a horse, Miles?' she asked.

He looked at the scribble, then looked speculatively at her, giving himself time to decide on the best attitude to adopt 'Yes, it's a horse,' he said at last.

Miranda began to chant, 'Silly, silly, silly!'

'It's a horse in an aeroplane,' Miles said.

'Round one to Miles,' Sam said from behind the newspaper that he had picked up to disguise his intentness on what was happening.

At that point Robina turned the picture over. 'It's a funny piece of paper,' she said. 'Where did you find it?'

Miles looked vague. 'I found it,' he said.

'I wonder where?' Robina said.

She tried to say it casually. She was sure she said it casually, yet something in her tone must have given Miles a warning that her interest was stronger than she wanted it to appear, and troubled a faintly uneasy conscience. The candour went out of his eyes, and he made a great show of balancing himself on one foot before he answered.

'I don't remember where,' he said. 'It's just an old piece of paper.'

'Did you find it in the house?' Robina asked.

He nodded.

Miranda gave a giggle. 'D 'you know, Mummy he thought it was money. That's because he's so little he doesn't know money's green.'

'Money's brown too,' Miles said.

Robina prayed for patience. 'Did you find it in this room?' she asked.

'Yes,' he said promptly. Too promptly. 'I found it—' He paused and looked round the room, all too probably trying to decide on a good place in which to claim that he had found the money. 'I found it in the chair.' He pointed at the chair in which Sam was sitting.

Sam at once stood up and was turning to examine the chair when Robina caught his eye and slightly shook her head.

'He always hides things in chairs himself,' she said. 'Well, it doesn't matter, anyway. It's only an old piece of paper.' She stood up and started to clear the breakfast.

Miles immediately regretted the loss of interest in himself. Standing on one foot again and swinging the other foot backwards and forwards in an airy way that would have overbalanced him if he had not clutched at Robina's skirt, he said, 'She gave it to me.'

'She?' Robina said.

He nodded, seeming to think that that information at last should be sufficient.

'D'you mean . . . ?' Robina hesitated. 'D'you mean Mrs Birch?' she asked.

'No,' he said.

'Mrs Booker?'

He looked a little shocked. 'The picture's *for* Mrs Booker,' he said. He knew that you did not return to people presents that they had given you.

'Iris, then?'

'No no no,' Miranda sang out, dancing about in a sudden ecstasy of amusement at the silliness of everybody. 'He means the witch, the three-footed witch!'

'The three-footed witch, the three-footed witch!' Miles suddenly yelled at the top of his voice and began spinning round and round as fast as he could with his arms held straight out on either side of him.

Sam clutched his head. 'Witchcraft! That's all that was needed. In God's name, what made them think of a thing like that?'

'It's a story Martha was telling them,' Robina said helplessly.

'Martha!' The name gave Sam an idea. Turning from the madly spinning Miles, he spoke to Miranda. 'That's whom he means, isn't it? Martha—the lady who spent the night here, sleeping on the sofa. He doesn't know she's called Mrs Birch.'

Miranda shrieked with laughter. 'He means the three-footed witch!' she cried and, bending down, put both hands on the floor, stuck one leg up in the air behind her and began a three-legged scuttle across the room, colliding with Miles, who had just collapsed on the carpet, panting and giddy.

As they rolled together on the floor the doorbell rang.

Sam snatched up the picture, thrust it into a pocket and went to the door. Outside, a figure looking abnormally large against the background of thick white fog, was Inspector Morton.

Morton said that the morning was cold and that the fog was very unpleasant, but he did not sound very convincing about it. It was as if he allowed the cold and the fog to affect his real feelings no more than murder. Quiet, unemphatic, clothed in his defensive armour of detachment, he came into the house, said good morning to Robina and smiled at the children. He said that something had come up which made him want to make sure that he had understood correctly a piece of information that he had been given the day before.

Sam's manner became what Robina thought Morton must have found unreasonably apologetic. But Morton did not know that Sam had a way of believing that he owed apologies to other people for his hard feelings about them, even when they had no suspicion of the feelings. For an hour or so the day before he had hated Morton and the feeling had sickened him. This morning, therefore, in his careful friendliness, he was trying to protect himself against a recurrence of that unreasoning hatred, which he recognized as the product of nothing but his own fears and an automatic resentment of authority.

Besides that, there was the picture in his pocket.

When Robina had sent the children out of the room Morton said, 'It's about that hatchet. I think you said that Ringrose couldn't have taken it. Are you sure that's a fact?'

'We can't be absolutely sure about it,' Robina said, 'but I don't think he could have taken it.'

'Because you left it outside your back door and Ringrose never went there.'

'Yes.'

'That's a complication,' Morton said. He sounded tired of complications.

'You said something has come up,' Sam said. 'Is it about Ringrose?'

'Ringrose has disappeared,' Morton answered. 'Sometime yesterday. His wife got in touch with us late last night. She

146

said he'd gone into Blanebury yesterday with the van. He does a vegetable round there on Fridays, and she was expecting him back in the late afternoon. He didn't turn up at the usual time, but she didn't start really worrying till the evening. We made some enquiries and found he'd done his round. But after that there's no trace of him or his van. You see what that could mean, of course.'

'I think I see,' Sam said cautiously.

'As we were saying yesterday,' Morton went on, 'when the worm turns on the blackmailer he can be a danger. And Ringrose was blackmailing Birch about Booker's death. Or so Mrs Ringrose says. She was in a state of breakdown by the evening, pouring out everything she knew or claimed to know. I think she's been under a great strain for a long time, a quite good sort of woman really, who's been trying to convince herself that there was good in her husband. And as long as he stuck to her, I dare say she'd have gone on convincing herself quite successfully, but once she thought he'd cleared out, taking the money he'd got from Birch, she let it all boil up.' He gave Robina a mildly quizzical glance. 'You went to see her yesterday, didn't you, Mrs Mellanby? I think that started the process. It seems to have been a relief of sorts to find that someone besides herself knew of her husband's activities.'

'She was very angry with me,' Robina said.

'Of course,' he said. 'Wouldn't you have been?'

'Then you think,' Sam said, 'that Ringrose murdered Birch, perhaps because Birch threatened to expose him, and then, realizing that his attempt to blackmail me had misfired and that he was probably going to be exposed anyhow, cleared out with the five hundred pounds.'

'It's a possibility, isn't it?'

'Except that . . .'

Except, Robina thought, as Sam stopped, that the five hundred pounds had never been intended for Ringrose, but for Pete.

Sam went on, 'I was going to say, except for the hatchet.'

Morton nodded. Of course he had noticed Sam changing his mind about what he was going to say. 'I'm sorry for that woman,' he said. 'She'd nothing to live for except her husband—no children, no friends, no interests. And frightened of everything. There are a lot of people like that. And they'll stand anything, even murder, from the person who props them up, except being let down themselves. If that happens to them they lose the only thing they've been able to believe in. You never quite know what they'll do then.'

'But she didn't believe he was a murderer,' Robina said.

'She didn't yesterday,' he answered. 'She does now, because he's left her. Of course that isn't evidence—in the sense that being able to show that he'd got hold of your hatchet would be evidence.'

He waited, looking from Sam to Robina, as if he hoped that the suggestion contained in his last phrase might stimulate some useful thought in one or other of their minds. They looked at one another and each saw a warning in the eyes of the other, a warning which was in itself an imprudence, under the calm gaze of Inspector Morton. Sam turned his head away and took a long, thoughtful look through the fog-shrouded window.

'Inspector, when I came to see you yesterday . . .' he said.

'Yes, Dr Mellanby.'

'I came to tell you that I'd lied.' He made an effort, turning again to look directly into Morton's eyes. 'But you seemed to know it already. Isn't that so?'

'I thought it likely,' Morton said.

'But you told me you hadn't seen Ringrose.'

'No. At that time he was on his vegetable round.'

'Am I right, then, in thinking that it was the book Birch appears to have been reading when he was killed that led you to think I'd been to the house? A book of mine, that had my name on the flyleaf.'

'You said *appears* to have been reading,' Morton said.

'I did. It's what I meant. Birch wasn't reading that book.'

'What was he doing with it then?'

'He wasn't doing anything. Someone put that book there after the murder, to make it look as if he'd been reading when he was killed. You thought he'd been reading, didn't you, reading in the daylight, with his back to the window? And that made you think that the murder was done around four or half past—the time when I was in the house. And that's the reason why I lied, because I knew you'd think that. But if I'd known what the book was I shouldn't have troubled to lie.'

'You have a reason for saying this, I suppose,' Morton said.

'A good and simple reason. Birch wasn't a scientist. To the best of my knowledge he hadn't a vestige of interest in science. And no one but a scientist would ever have attempted to read that book. If you doubt that, try to read it yourself.'

'I have,' Morton said. 'I don't doubt it.'

'Yet I see that you doubt my conclusion.'

Morton brought the tips of his fingers together and looked at them dispassionately, as if they too were evidence connected with the murder of Douglas Birch. They seemed not quite to satisfy him. 'It's an interesting point,' he said, 'a point worth considering. At present I wouldn't go further than that. You did take that book into the house, I suppose?'

'I must have done'

'Just why?'

'I don't know. Automatically, I think. I often do absent-minded things, particularly when I'm worried, and I was worried at the thought of the interview with Birch. I'd been meaning to take the book out of the car when I got home, and I just did it too soon.'

'And then forgot it?'

'Yes.'

'I know one does that sort of thing,' Morton said. 'All the same, I doubt if you've proved anything. Birch need not have been reading that book when he was killed. He could merely have picked it up out of curiosity and been taking a look at it when the murderer struck him. Still, it's an interesting point, as I said. Is there any special reason why you brought it up just now?'

Sam was growing restless. Robina thought that the same feelings that had attacked him during his interview with Morton the day before were troubling him now. But if so, he was still holding his increasing antagonism in check.

'I'm afraid if my theory about that book doesn't impress you,' he said, 'my reason for bringing it up won't either. It was this. Assuming for the sake of argument that I was right that that book was put on Birch's knee to make it appear that he was reading at the time of his murder, then whoever put it there was making a blunder, picking just the one book in the room that Birch couldn't have been reading. And that suggests it must have been someone who didn't really know much about Birch, or about books, or about science.'

'In other words, not yourself, or Mrs Birch, or Dr Hillman, or Dr Ovenden—and probably not Mrs Swinson or Miss Swinson.' Parenthetically he added, 'I'm just going over the people who conceivably could have taken your hatchet.'

'Exactly,' Sam said.

'So we get back to Ringrose.'

'Well, it's an interesting point,' Sam said, 'a point worth considering. At present I wouldn't go further than that.'

Morton smiled good-naturedly at the parody. 'It is at that,' he said. 'I'll think it over. But I think there could be other explanations of the situation. As I said, Birch could have picked the book up out of casual curiosity. Or the murderer—an oversubtle murderer—might even have handed him the book, saying, "Take a look at this," to produce precisely the appearances you've described to me. Or he might have been the sort of character that gets a bit flustered when he commits a murder and makes an occasional mistake. The best of us make a mistake some-times—' He broke off as the telephone rang.

To Robina it was a relief. She was nervous of the response that Sam might make to the insinuations in Morton's speech. She saw that the colour in his cheeks had deepened a little. But he managed to speak quietly into the telephone, and then, holding it out to Morton, to say easily, 'For you, Inspector.'

Robina's relief was short-lived. As soon as Morton put the instrument to his ear she saw that something had gone desperately wrong. For once his mask of detachment cracked across and she saw for an instant an angry and violent man, off his guard.

'Don't go!' he barked at her and Sam as they were going to the door, to let him hold his conversation in private.

They heard the rasp of the voice at the other end of the line. Morton himself said little, but all the time that the other voice went on he kept his eyes on Sam. He seemed to be looking straight through him, yet when Sam moved the eyes followed him.

At last Morton put the telephone down. 'Ringrose and his van have been found at the bottom of Fyes quarry, about a mile from here,' he said. 'Ringrose is dead.'

At that moment there was a scream in the hall.

It was a scream of mortal terror, a sound not unfamiliar and only moderately disturbing to Robina and Sam. But Morton swung round as if he had been struck. The door flew open and Miranda tore into the room. Her face was white, her eyes were glazed with tears and panic and her arms were flung out to clutch at safety.

'Miles is in the wardrobe!' she shrieked. 'He climbed inside to find the three-footed witch—and he can't get out

—and I know we'll never see him again!' Sobbing and shaking, she clung to Robina.

It was Morton who seemed relieved now. The interruption gave him the chance to readjust his mask, without which he would rapidly have become a nervous and incompetent officer, his anger and violence being those of a sensitive man who had never learnt to like the relationships with other people that were forced on him by his work.

'I'm sure it's not as bad as all that,' he said, strode out into the hall and wrenched open the door of the wardrobe.

Miles was standing upright inside it. His face was also a little pale, though he had faced his dangers with greater calm than Miranda. He was holding something in both hands and, expecting to see Sam, held it out to him.

Seeing a stranger, he immediately pulled it back. In doing so, his hold on it slipped, and a shower of five-pound notes slid from his hands onto the floor at Inspector Morton's feet.

CHAPTER 16

It was a few minutes later that the other policemen came, but it was more than an hour before they took Sam away. Of that time, and the time that immediately followed it, Robina remembered almost nothing. It became fused in her mind with another time in her life, so that afterwards she always felt sure that certain things had happened that in fact could not possibly have happened.

For instance, a most trivial thing, whenever she visualized the scene she always saw herself as wearing a black and white tweed coat. Yet, since she was indoors, she had naturally not been wearing a coat at all. Besides, that coat had been cut down years before to make a coat for Miranda.

As well as that, it always seemed to her that a woman in

the white uniform of a nurse had been present at the time of Sam's arrest. But really there had been no woman in the house besides herself and Mrs Booker.

The children, particularly Miranda, had a strange half understanding of what was happening, and went wild with terror in a total and appalling certainty of loss. Miranda always had this fear somewhere in the back of her mind and from time to time, even when everything else was calm, would become so convinced that someone who had just gone out of the room would never come back again that she would start to cry and scream in a panic that appeared to have no reason. On these occasions Miles sometimes thought it fitting to imitate her, and today, for a long time after the police had gone, Robina had two sobbing, white-faced children following her and holding onto her wherever she went.

She saw, in a way, that the police could hardly have done other than they had. The weapon that had killed Douglas Birch had come from this house. The missing money had been found in it. Sam had been in the Birches' house at the time the police believed the murder to have been committed and at first had lied about this. And he had, they believed, a motive. Useless for Robina to tell them that he had no motive. If they believed that she herself believed what she was saying, they might be sorry for her, but would not be convinced.

So far as she could tell, they had learnt nothing specific to link Sam with Ringrose's murder, except that he had been seen talking to Ringrose in Blanebury the afternoon before and that this talk had been acrimonious. Ringrose had shouted at Sam and had been heard to say that he had been given fair warning. Sam had answered that Ringrose had better look out for himself. But the weapon that had been used to stun Ringrose before the murderer pushed him out of the driver's seat of his van and drove the van to the quarry belonged to Ringrose himself. It was a heavy hoe that he had bought in Blanebury only that afternoon.

The police theory was that Ringrose had given a lift to his murderer, or else that while he was delivering his last vegetables in Blanebury, or during some later stop that he had made, the murderer had hidden in the van, finding there the hoe and using it rather than some weapon that he had brought with him, the ownership of which might be traced.

How it happened Robina did not know, but almost as soon as Sam's arrest had taken place it seemed to be widely known in Burnham Priors. Perhaps, she thought, it had been far more generally expected than she had dreamt. From the windows she saw little groups of people gather in the road, staring and pointing.

After only a short time Edna Swinson pedalled furiously on her bicycle and, seeing these people, did her best to drive them away, abusing them in a loud, angry voice. The groups melted a little, but re-formed.

Coming into the house, Edna tried to persuade Robina to come away with her. 'You can't stay here like this,' she said. 'Get the children, pop in the car and come straight along. I'll fit you all in somehow and Mrs Booker can look after things here. Now don't argue.' Her ruddy cheeks were redder than usual and there was a glitter of tears in her eyes. 'The fools, the wicked fools!' she shouted, strident and clumsy in her rage.

But Robina would not be persuaded. An intense rage was burning inside her as well. She was grateful to Edna, but at the same time impatient for her to leave. Except for Mrs Booker, whose presence in some unexpected way she found reassuring, she wanted the house to herself and the children. If there had been bolts and bars to fix over the doors and the windows she probably would have put them up, making it clear to all that this was her home and that she was defending it until her husband's return. To have left the house would have felt like admitting defeat at the outset.

Besides that, Robina found something happening to her which made her want to keep everyone at arm's length. It was something that had never happened before and that made her wonder if her mind had not been so jarred by the calamity that she had become, at least for the time being, a little crazed.

The trouble was a flood of distrust washing into every corner of her being. She found herself looking at Edna, with her hot cheeks, blazing eyes and earrings fiercely swinging with the angry jerks of her head, and thinking, 'It could have been you! It could have been even you who did two murders and coldly, relentlessly, falsified the evidence of your own crime so that Sam should suffer for it!'

As soon as Edna had left, Robina felt great shame for these thoughts. But it was no use now, she thought allowing feelings like shame, or memories of many kindnesses, or the habits of friendship, to blind her to the fact that someone was trying, with cold deliberation, to make Sam pay for his crimes, and that that person, almost for certain, since no one else could have stolen the hatchet or hidden the money in the wardrobe, was either Edna, or Iris, or Martha, or Pete, or Denis.

Trying to keep her mind unprejudiced by her feelings for them, she set about making out a case against each of these, seeing what it amounted to. But she was too desperate and too tired to think with any clarity. All the time her feelings intervened, upsetting her thinking so that the fact that she liked Edna and Pete too much, and Martha too little, made nonsense of her attempts to compare justly their potentialities for murder.

About Iris and Denis she was able to think a little more dispassionately. Here were two people of whom, in reality, she knew very little. When she examined her feelings about them she found that they had been formed mostly by what she had been told by Sam. Yet she knew of no reason whatever why Iris should hate either Douglas or Sam, though Denis, if he had discovered that it was Douglas who had killed Booker and allowed him to take the blame, might just conceivably have been so filled with hatred that he could have murdered Douglas. But would he cold-bloodedly have planted his guilt on Sam? Would he have stolen five hundred pounds?

Besides, where did the missing ice cubes come in? Who had been to the house that afternoon and had a drink with Douglas, a drink sufficiently leisurely for ice to have been put in it?

It was in the middle of the afternoon that Inspector Morton reappeared.

When Robina opened the door he did not greet her, and as she let him come in he did not speak. This seemed a kind of absent-mindedness, rather than intentional. He seemed to be following a train of thought and to be afraid that if he did not follow it to a conclusion he might lose it altogether.

When he went into the sitting-room he walked to the window. The fog had not quite gone, though it was not nearly as dense as in the morning. It was possible to see the trees on the far side of the road, and such cars as passed no longer had their lights on. But Morton, as he stood peering out into the mist, looked as if he could see no farther than he had earlier.

Robina hurriedly sent the unwilling children out to Mrs Booker. But even when they had gone Morton still said nothing. He only turned and looked at Robina.

She thought, of all absurd things, that he looked resentful, as if he suspected her of having done him an injury, and he still seemed to be sunk deep in his own thoughts.

At last she exclaimed, 'If it's only a quiet think you want, do you have to have it here?'

He looked startled. 'No. That is . . . Look here, Mrs Mellanby, who hated your husband?' He rapped the question out at her as peremptorily as if she had been refusing to answer questions for an hour.

She dropped into a chair. 'Naturally I've been asking myself that,' she said.

'Put it like this.' Now he sounded as if he were talking to himself, arguing with himself. 'There's evidence against him. A good deal. Enough, probably. And this idea he's got that someone's been faking the evidence against him, there isn't much to support it. A book. The wrong book for Birch to have been reading. That isn't much. You've got to admit it isn't much. You can explain it as I explained it this morning. On the other hand . . .' He paused, put the top joint of his thumb in his mouth and bit it fiercely. 'I don't like to make mistakes,' he said.

Excitement had kindled in Robina. 'Do you make so many?' she asked.

'Enough,' he said. 'Everyone does. And most people hate the memory of them, if only out of vanity, though that isn't always the only reason.'

'I don't think you're an awfully vain man,' she said.

'What do you know about it?' he asked quickly. 'And what do I know about your husband, except that . . . except that I smell a mistake. There's something wrong. He hasn't got the smell of murder about him. There's a lot of evidence against him and all he has to say about it is that somebody faked it. That's what anyone in his shoes would say. And all he has to say in support of that is that Birch was reading the wrong sort of book. But it was Mellanby himself who took that book into the house, for no good reason.'

'You said yourself one does that sort of thing,' Robina said.

'Oh yes, one does, easily. Particularly an absent-minded scientist. Aren't scientists absent-minded? Scientists, philosophers, all the rest of them—doesn't the popular view of them give them a wonderful alibi for anything odd they choose to do?'

'Aren't you ever absent-minded yourself?' she asked.

157

'Of course I am,' he barked at her. 'But who'd make allowances for that in my job?'

'Your wife, anyway,' she suggested.

For the first time he smiled. 'What wives think about their husbands doesn't carry much weight in a court of law —except sometimes a divorce court.'

'All the same, I believe you've come here mostly to find out what I think about my husband,' Robina said.

'We're getting away from the point,' he said. 'That book we were talking about. He admits he took it into the house himself and left it there. Then he claims that someone else put it on Birch's lap after he'd killed him, the idea being to make it look as if Birch was reading by daylight when he was killed. And he claims that no one who knew anything of Birch or of the book would ever have chosen that particular book for that purpose. He comes out very pat with that suggestion. Then he points out that, of all the people we've been thinking about as possible murderers, only Ringrose wouldn't have known enough to make that mistake. And Ringrose is dead, conceivably a suicide. If the van had gone on fire when it went over into the quarry there'd be no proof he wasn't a suicide. So the suggestion, as I understand it, is that Ringrose did the murder, faked the evidence to incriminate Mellanby, then tried to blackmail him. But finding that he was a tougher nut to crack in that respect than Birch had been, and that he was going to come to us with the facts, lost his head and committed suicide. Isn't that how it's supposed to hang together—and all because of a book that Mellanby took into the house himself?'

'You know,' Robina said, 'that's much too subtle, even for Sam.'

'"Even for Sam!" He pounced on the phrase with a sound of triumph. Jerking a chair forward, he sat down on the edge of it, leaning towards her. 'Now aren't we getting somewhere? Absent-minded he may be, for all I know, but isn't he subtle too? In my experience, intellectual types like your husband *are* oversubtle as soon as they go in for action. They think out too much in advance. They try to cover too many possibilities. They forget that the best way to get away with a thing is to hit out and run.'

'No,' Robina said. 'All this subtlety's your own—and you don't believe in it, or you wouldn't be here now.'

He leant back. Tilting his head, he stared moodily at the ceiling.

'No, I don't,' he muttered. 'Either the evidence in that room was real, in which case your husband's guilty, or it was faked by someone else, in which case there's someone around among his friends who hates him. So we come back to what I asked you first. Who hates him, Mrs Mellanby?'

She did not try to answer. She did not think he wanted an answer. She thought that he had come here to talk himself, to experiment in talk with his own thoughts.

After a moment he went on, 'Take Martha Birch. She'd motive and opportunity. She'd make a good suspect. And perhaps she hated your husband. I don't know about that.'

He brought his gaze back from the ceiling, meeting Robina's eyes and cocking an eyebrow at her, and though he had not asked a question, she realized that this time he expected an answer.

'Opportunity?' she said.

'Oh yes, didn't you know about that?' he said. 'While you were calling on Mrs Ringrose, Mrs Birch went out.'

'Has she said so?' she asked, astonished.

'No, she says that she didn't go out. But I've spoken to Darley, the man who delivered some logs to you, and he says that he couldn't get any answer when he knocked here. He knocked at the front and the back and there was no answer. Mrs Birch's explanation is that she heard him, but that she's afraid of opening doors after dark. I don't know how that strikes you.'

'It could be true,' Robina said.

He brought both hands down with a slap on his knees.

'Have I come here to listen to you being impartial and fair-minded? *What do you believe?*'

She flushed. 'I want to believe that she went out,' she said. 'But you see she really had no reason to kill Douglas. Really she hadn't.'

'Why are you so sure?'

'Because . . . well, I don't know if I can make it clear, but if she was tired of him and wanted to leave him, perhaps to marry somebody else, and if he wouldn't divorce her, that really wouldn't upset her so terribly. I'm sure it wouldn't. She'd simply have left him and not worried too much about what anyone said about it.'

'Yes,' Morton said, 'you're probably right. But there's always money, isn't there?'

'Not a great deal, you know. There's the house, of course. I suppose it's worth five or six thousand. But from things I've heard them say, I think they lived up to their income, and that all came from Douglas's writing, so it won't go on. No, I really can't see Martha committing a murder for the sake of respectability and six thousand pounds. And then there's another thing—'

'Wait a minute,' he said. 'I think I know what you're going to say. You're going to say that even if she did, even if she took your hatchet with her and killed her husband, she hadn't time for the rest of it. Not that it would have taken more than a moment to dump the book on Birch's lap, turn off the lamp and draw back the curtains. But to be able to think of that when you've just committed a murder, that's the point, isn't it? Because she couldn't have thought it out in advance. She couldn't have known where her husband would be sitting, or even that he'd be in that room at all. At that time of day he was usually out for a walk.'

Robina sat up with a start. 'Of course he was! I hadn't thought of that. But then . . .'

'Then, if she killed him, as I was saying, she hadn't got

it all thought out in advance. She just made use of an unexpected opportunity. But if she managed to do the rest of it, when she knew you might return home at any moment and find her gone, she's a more remarkable woman than I think her.'

Robina sighed. 'I know. It won't do, will it?'

He waited, as if he hoped that she might have more to say. When she remained silent, he echoed her sigh. 'Look, I'm doing my best,' he said.

'I know,' she said. 'I'm grateful.'

'Isn't there anything you can tell me—anything at all? For instance, when you went out to call on Mrs Ringrose, did you say anything that could have given Mrs Birch any idea of how long you'd be?'

'I'm sure I didn't.'

Again he waited. Then he stood up. 'I'll tell you something,' he said. 'Something about Ringrose. I don't know yet what it means, or if it means anything. When his body was found there was an odd thing in one of his pockets. Tea leaves!'

She looked at him stupidly. 'Tea leaves—in his pocket?'

'Yes, in a matchbox. Still a bit damp. China tea. The Ringroses don't drink China tea. The Birches do. Does that suggest anything to you?'

She put her hands to her head. 'I'm sorry,' she said, 'I can hardly manage to think at all. At the moment—tea leaves! It sounds like idiocy. But perhaps when you're gone, when I've had some time . . . I'm grateful to you for coming. I'm much more grateful than I sound. I think since this morning I've been stopped dead—everything in me run down. But now perhaps I'll start going again. I'll think about these things you've asked me, and perhaps . . . But about Martha Birch—' She raised her head and looked at him. 'I don't honestly believe she hates Sam. I'd like to say I think she does, but I don't. I know it was she who persuaded him to go to see her husband, but she couldn't know what time he'd go, or even for certain that he'd go at all. He didn't want to. If she did do this murder and then change things around to give herself an alibi, then I don't think she ever meant to involve Sam. He just got in the way by chance, and she's probably sorry for it. Only, of course, she couldn't really have done it.'

'And you can't name anyone else who hates your husband?'

She shook her head helplessly. 'Whoever it is has covered it very successfully—if there is such a person.'

'Most people have stirred up hatred sometime in their lives,' he said, 'even if they never find it out. Husbands, wives, brothers, sisters, colleagues—they all make good haters. Secret haters.'

She stood up, facing him. 'You don't really like your job, do you?'

He seemed taken by surprise. 'What makes you think that? There's a great fascination in it. You don't understand that? Oh, a great fascination. The fascination of evil. We all feel it, you know. Only it isn't always plain sailing. Well, goodbye, Mrs Mellanby. Get in touch with me whenever you want to.' He left, all of a sudden in a hurry.

As soon as he had gone Robina found she wished that he had stayed longer. So long as he was there she had had the feeling of doing something and, curiously enough, of being protected from the groups of people, hostile or merely inquisitive, that formed, dispersed and re-formed outside. At least she had forgotten about them. Now, once more, she became acutely conscious of them, and her cheeks burned and her skin prickled as she caught glimpses of them through the window.

She started to think over what she had told Morton about Martha. She had no love for Martha. At most, she had an uneasy sort of sympathy with her. Marriage with Douglas must have had grave disadvantages. Not for the first time Robina found herself wondering what it was that had made Martha leave Sam for him. Money? Fame? Douglas was only moderately rich and moderately famous. But perhaps Martha had not realized that. And perhaps she had thought that Douglas, immersed in his work and his dreams, would make an easygoing, complacent husband, a factor possibly of importance to one of her temperament. Then again, perhaps she had simply fallen in love with him. On the whole, that seemed the best explanation. Fallen in love with him, then out of love with him, then in love with somebody else, all quite incomprehensibly to anyone but herself.

To herself it would probably have seemed that each new love was the result of a wise discrimination, promising release from past frustrations and forgetfulness of old disappointments. And so it would be with the next love and the next.

It took women like Martha a long time to recognize that for the most part they were helplessly controlled by a pattern of desires that they did not understand and which caused them over and over again to make the same mistakes. Which was all very well, Robina thought, and sounded quite impressive, but it did not tell her the identity of Martha's present mistake, if it was not Pete Hillman. And who it was would be worth knowing, because he was probably the murderer of Douglas Birch.

'Mrs Booker!' Robina called out suddenly and went running out to the kitchen. 'Mrs Booker, I've just thought of something. I want to go and have a talk with Miss Woods. I shan't be long.'

'That's all right, dear,' Mrs Booker answered. 'It's about the ice, I suppose.'

'Why, no,' Robina said. 'It's about something else—something she might know, as she lived in that house.'

'I've been thinking about the ice,' Mrs Booker said. 'I keep thinking about the ice, wondering what I could have done with it myself if I'd been there, if you see what I mean. That's the way I always act when something's lost. I ask, "If I was my old man, where would I have put it?" Or, "If

I was Miss Harber—" that's the old lady I've been going to on Wednesdays for the last thirteen years, and she's always losing things and getting in quite a state about it— "if I was Miss Harber, where would I have put it?" And if it was my old man, the thing was always in the pocket where he never put anything, *never*, so he said. And if it's Miss Harber, she's left it in the car, that she hasn't been out in for days, so it couldn't be there. You see what I mean. And so I've been thinking of the ice and all the people who never have ice in their drinks. I couldn't say I've got the answer, but I'm thinking about it. Where would *I* have put that ice? And I've been remembering an American gentleman I used to look after in the war, who never touched spirits at any time, not even when he had lumbago. I told him, "What you want is a nice hot rum," I said, "hot rum with just a pinch of bicarbonate of soda and a clove, it'll loosen off the muscles," I said. But he wouldn't touch it. What he liked to drink all the time was iced tea. You'll never believe how he used to tell me to make that tea . . .'

She rambled on. At some point in the middle of it Robina turned quietly and went out.

She walked quietly, her manner was quiet. She looked down at the ground before her. Mrs Booker could have had no suspicion of the excitement that had suddenly set her heart pounding, of the understanding that had suddenly come.

Not that Douglas had been drinking iced tea when he was killed, or that anyone else had been drinking it.

CHAPTER 17

Robina had thought of going the short distance to the Birches' house by car. This was because of the people she expected to find in the road. But because the fog had grown thicker again there was no one there. The chill damp had driven them all home to their fires.

Changing her mind, she set out on foot. Ahead, where the road dropped slightly downhill, a dense grey-white cloud seemed to rest on the road. It concealed the contours of the hedges, with which she was beginning to grow familiar, and it seemed to her an unusually long time before she reached the Birches' gates. Beginning to wonder if she could have passed them by, she came on them suddenly, finding them closed and fastened with a padlock.

This took her aback. She had forgotten that Miss Woods had spoken of going to stay with a married sister. Probably she was at her sister's home now, leaving everything here locked and bolted. Yet there was a light in the house, shining dimly through the fog.

Robina took hold of the top bar of the gate. It was a high gate, but not difficult to climb. In a moment she was trotting on up the drive. She arrived at the door panting and with her heart beating fast and, as she rang the bell, wondered if she would find only the police in possession. The sound of a light footstep inside reassured her. The door was opened and she found herself face to face with Martha.

Robina realized that she ought not to have felt so surprised. This was Martha's home. The surprise that she saw on Martha's face was better justified. Surprise, however, was not all that Robina saw there, or so she instantly imagined. She had the feeling that Martha had been expecting someone else and that the first expression that came into her eyes was sharp annoyance.

But almost at once Martha thrust out an arm, put it round Robina's shoulders and drew her inside.

'I was coming to see you,' she said. 'I wanted to tell you —I wanted to say—oh, how can I say it? But you know what I mean. It couldn't have been Sam. Some impossible mistake's been made.' She looked very white under the hall lamp, with heavy shadows under her eyes. She was dressed in black. 'How did you know I was here?' she asked.

'I didn't,' Robina said. 'I wanted to see Miss Woods.'

'She isn't here. I sent her a message, asking her to come back, and when I heard you ring I thought that was who it might be. How did you manage about the padlock?'

'I climbed the gate.'

'I put it there because of the crowds. I expect you've had them too. You're close to the road, so perhaps they didn't actually force their way into your garden to look at you. Come in here.' Martha opened the door of the drawing-room.

But as Robina went into the room Martha went back to the front door. Robina heard it slam. Then Martha followed her into the drawing-room.

'It's all horribly cold,' she said. 'The central heating's been turned off. I've turned it on again, but the place hasn't warmed up yet.'

The room was a pretty one, all light colours and delicate shapes and usually with a great many flowers in it. The vases were there now but all were empty. At the moment, that made the room seem all the more desolate.

'Don't you mind being here on your own?' Robina asked.

'I hate it!' Martha said. 'But I couldn't stay on at the Swinsons'. It was bad enough when they all thought I'd murdered Douglas, but now . . .' Her face crumpled as if she were going to cry.

Robina crossed to a radiator and laid her cold hands upon it. She was thinking that there were several things wrong with what Martha had been saying to her. For instance, why should she have expected Miss Woods to ring the bell? As housekeeper, Miss Woods would certainly have a key of the house. But it was not likely that she would be carrying around with her a key of the padlock that had been put on the gate only that afternoon, so if Martha had been surprised at Robina's climbing the gate, how had she expected Miss Woods to get into the garden?

What it amounted to was that the person whom Martha had been expecting had not been Miss Woods.

'Why is it worse now?' she asked.

'Because they all hate me,' Martha said. 'They all act as if it's somehow my fault that I'm *not* guilty.'

'I'm sure that's imagination,' Robina said.

'You know it isn't,' Martha said, 'because it's how you feel yourself. But in you I understand it. I don't mind it. In a way I feel I even deserve it. But in the others, even if they care for Sam so much more than me, it's—' her voice trembled—'it's horrible. I'm terrified of this house, but I can bear it much better than I can those awful faces.'

'You think everyone hates you,' Robina said. 'I wonder why?'

'I don't. That is, I've only just found out. And only those people. Usually I feel that I can make people like me, when I want to. But now something's gone all wrong and I feel helpless and miserable, just when I most need help. I'm not tough like you. I haven't got your courage.' Martha's face was crumpling again with the threat of tears.

'You've more courage than you like to let on about,' Robina said.

'I don't know what you mean,' Martha said.

'I was thinking about your answering the door just now,' Robina said. 'You were too frightened to open our door to Mr Darley.'

'But I thought you were Miss Woods.' Martha looked anxiously into Robina's face, as if she found something disturbing in her expression, then unexpectedly her own expression changed. The intensity went out of it and she almost smiled. 'You're perfectly right not to believe me, of course. It was really someone else I was expecting.'

'I didn't believe you about Mr Darley either,' Robina said. She was a little puzzled at her own behaviour and her own feelings. She could hear how calm she sounded. It was an entirely artificial calm, yet she was not conscious of making any effort to produce it. Rather it was as if this calm were not a part of herself but had taken possession of her. It was a frightening feeling. 'You did go out that evening, didn't you?' she said. 'When I came in, with Sam and Pete, you already knew that Douglas was dead.'

She saw the motion of one of Martha's hands, which she was lifting to her head, arrested in mid-air. Then Martha turned away and walked across the room to the fireplace. It had a high marble chimney piece. She leant against it, a tall, slender figure in black, sharply outlined against the white marble.

'What makes you believe that?' she asked. There was wonder in her voice.

'Because you couldn't hide your joy,' Robina said.

'That's a fearful thing to say.'

'I know it is.'

'And that's your whole reason for saying it—that you assume I'd show delight at Douglas's death?'

'That and your unconvincing story about Mr Darley.'

'I see. But why don't you say the rest of it? Why don't you say that I came over here and murdered Douglas?'

'Because I don't see how you could have done,' Robina said.

Martha turned slowly. She also seemed to have been infected by the false calm that had control of Robina. There was a sort of lassitude in her movement. But her grey-blue eyes, with the dark rims round the irises, were vivid with a glitter of mockery in them. 'I didn't expect that,' she said. 'I thought you had it all worked out.'

'Not all of it.'

'And I didn't murder my husband?'

'If you did,' Robina said, 'someone worked hard and fast to cover up the traces for you. Who would have done that?'

'I'd like to know. At the moment I'd be glad to know of anyone who'd do anything for me.'

'Of course there's still this man for whom you wanted to

leave Douglas. You told Sam and me about him, remember? Wouldn't he do anything for you?'

'He?' Martha gave a short, desperate laugh. 'He thinks I killed Douglas, and each time he looks at me he lets me see that the most he'll do for me is keep his thoughts to himself. And now that they've arrested Sam, I don't trust him to do even that. I've been a fool, an utter fool! I always make a fool of myself about men. I've got no sense, no understanding.'

'So he minds about Sam's arrest or you think he does,' Robina said.

Martha made a fretful gesture. 'Let's keep to the subject, or you'll get me too confused. You were telling me why I couldn't have murdered my husband. I'd be glad to know. It might come in useful.'

'It isn't because you didn't come over here,' Robina said. 'I believe you did and I believe you found Douglas dead. And even if grief or regret of a sort came later, I think your first feeling was delight in your freedom. That's why you looked at Pete as you did. Pete was an enemy. He'd been helping Douglas to get you away to America, away from your lover, and he'd failed and you were triumphing over him. It may amuse you to know that because of that little scene between you and Pete, with you sort of glowing and Pete looking so embarrassed, because he realized you knew he was trying to help Douglas, Sam and I jumped to the conclusion that Pete was the lover you'd spoken of. Or did you mean us to think that, to stop us thinking about anyone else?'

Martha ignored the question. 'Aren't you saying, if I found Douglas dead, that Sam must have killed him?'

'There was quite an interval between the time Sam left and the time you came here.'

'If you believe Sam.'

'Yes.'

'It must be pleasant to be believed occasionally,' Martha

said tonelessly. 'But I seem to remember that Sam told a number of lies.'

'That's true.'

'But on this point you choose to believe him.'

'Yes.'

'Well, go on,' Martha said. 'You still haven't got to the part that interests me.'

Robina moved away from the radiator. It was growing so hot now that she could not keep her hands on it, but the chill had not gone from the room, or even out of her hands. Thrusting them into her pockets, she began to walk restlessly about.

'It's the way that the scene was set, you see,' she said. 'Someone set the scene to make it look as if the murder had happened much earlier than it did. Whoever it was put a book on Douglas's knee, turned off the lamp and drew back the curtains. That was all to make it look as if Douglas had been reading by daylight when he was killed. Then the setting of the thermostat was changed, to make the room abnormally warm, so that it wouldn't be easy to tell from the state of the body how long Douglas had been dead.'

'And I didn't do these things?' Martha said.

'You might have—you just possibly might have,' Robina answered, 'but you couldn't have made the cold tea. You hadn't time for that. You didn't know how long I'd stay at the Ringroses', and if you'd done a murder you couldn't have risked my getting home again before you did. You wouldn't have stayed here, messing about with the tea.'

'Tea?' Martha said.

'The teapot was cold, you see, when Sam and Pete got here,' Robina said, 'and in a very warm room it takes a teapot quite a time to get really cold. What happened, I think, was this. Douglas had just made his tea when the murderer came, and the murderer realized that if someone came in and found the body while the teapot was still hot it would completely upset the picture he tried to build up of Douglas having been killed an hour or more before he really was. So the murderer took the teapot and probably the full teacup out to the kitchen and washed them out and dried them on the tea cloth—that's how it was used. But then it occurred to him that he didn't know where to put the tea things, and that it would have been better to leave the tray in the sitting-room, or something like that. So he made some fresh tea, using a very little boiling water, and then some ice cubes to cool it rapidly. Then he took the pot and the cup back to Douglas's room and set the scene as Miss Woods found it presently. But all that must have taken time. And you wouldn't, you couldn't have risked staying here long enough to do that. So unless someone came in here after you'd done the murder, and deliberately covered it up for you, you didn't do the murder.'

Martha drew a long breath. Turning suddenly, she crossed her arms on the mantelshelf and hid her face in them.

'But that doesn't mean I know the rest of it,' Robina said. 'That happened—I'm sure that happened—but who it was . . .' In her pockets, her hands clenched into fists. 'It ought to have been Ringrose, because they found some tea leaves in a matchbox in one of his pockets—and they were China tea too. You see, he might have been afraid of just throwing them away, in case they were noticed and made someone wonder why Douglas had made two pots of tea. And then there was the book that Douglas was supposed to be reading. The most likely person to have made that mistake was Ringrose. But Ringrose himself was murdered. And anyway, how did he get the hatchet? And what was his motive—either for murdering Douglas or helping you, if you'd done the murder? I don't believe it was just that Douglas had threatened to go to the police about his blackmailing activities. For one thing, I don't believe Douglas would ever have done that. And as to the other . . .'

Martha raised her head a little. 'I wonder you don't suggest that Ringrose was my lover.'

'I've thought about that,' Robina said. 'It would fit so many of the facts. Only there's an important one it doesn't fit. I met him and talked to him, and it's too big a strain on the imagination to see him as your lover. It just won't do.'

Martha turned round and looked at Robina. 'I admire you,' she said. 'I really do. It would have been so easy to accuse me of that. I know how you're feeling at the moment. I know that you're floundering around, trying to grasp at any straw. Yet somehow you keep your head, and though you'd be quite glad to throw me to the wolves you've actually worked out a sort of case in my defence.'

Robina stood still, meeting Martha's eyes. 'Why don't you tell me then what you really did that evening?' she said. 'Don't you see that it might help us all?'

'There's only one person it wouldn't help,' Martha answered.

'The murderer.'

'Sam.'

They went on looking at one another. Then Martha gave a shrug of her shoulders and, moving away from the fireplace, sat down in a low armchair. She leant back in it, folding her hands behind her head and again looking fixedly at Robina.

'All right, I'll tell you about it,' she said. 'If—if it's as dangerous to Sam as I think it is, no one need ever know it but you and me. The truth is, I did come over here. I came almost as soon as you went out. I did it on an impulse. Of course I knew I oughtn't to leave the children, but I meant to be only a few minutes, and they were quite quiet. I *was* only a few minutes.'

'Why did you come?' Robina asked.

'Because I thought Douglas would be out, on his usual walk, and I wanted some clothes and my handbag. And I was going to leave him a note, telling him that I was never

172

coming back. But when I got here . . .' She pulled one hand from under her head and laid it across her eyes, shutting out a remembered sight. 'I went straight to his room, you see, to make sure he wasn't there. But he *was* there. Just as Sam and Pete found him.'

'You mean the book and the tea tray . . . ?'

'Oh, I don't know about that. I can't remember any of the details. I've tried to, for Sam's sake. But I only remember Douglas there in the chair—and the hatchet—and the blood. I ran. I ran as fast as I could. I got back without being seen and I thought all I had to do was say that I hadn't been out. But that farmer had been with his wood while I was gone, and of course could say that he hadn't been able to get an answer when he knocked. So I made up the story about being too scared to open the door. I knew it wasn't very good, but I thought I just might be able to carry it off.'

'You never thought of simply telling the truth about what you'd seen?'

'How could I?'

'That's something I don't really understand,' Robina said. 'Why couldn't you? You say you'd already decided to leave Douglas. That means you'd decided you could get on without his money, and apart from his money, he'd no real power over you. So you'd no real motive.'

'But who would have believed that?' Martha sprang to her feet. It was she who now started to move restlessly about, while Robina stood still, watching her with concentration as she paced up and down.

'Who'd have believed that the money didn't matter to me?' Martha said. 'Who'd have believed that it didn't matter deeply to me that I couldn't marry the man I wanted?' Her voice had become harsh. 'Both those things did matter to me, that was the truth. Only not enough to do murder. But d'you think I could have made the police believe that? You, perhaps. Perhaps I could have made you and a few other people believe me. But not the police, or the newspapers, or a jury. I *had* to lie. And besides—besides that, I thought Sam was the murderer, and the truth, if it didn't destroy me, would have destroyed him. Don't you see that?' She gripped the back of a chair and give it a vicious jerk. 'Don't you see that?' she repeated shrilly.

The sound the chair made as it scraped across the floor mingled with another sound that Robina heard faintly, so faintly that she was not entirely sure that she had heard it. It was a sound that seemed to come from the hall. Caught unawares, she glanced towards the door, but then looked away and deliberately did not look in that direction again.

'Would you really mind much if Sam were destroyed?' she said.

'What d'you think?' Martha said. 'This is something you may not understand, but in a way I care more about Sam than any man I've ever known. If he'd cared more for me —me, as I am, I mean, and not a character he'd created in his mind, in comparison with whom he really despised me—if he'd done that, I'd never have given him up for Douglas.'

'But that's just what you said about Douglas,' Robina said, 'that he tried to make you be a person he'd invented.'

'Isn't it what all men do?'

'And all women too?' Robina had heard that sound again. This time she was sure that she had heard it and she was fairly sure that it was the sound of a foot being moved. She went on. 'It could easily have been the other way round all the time, I mean that it was the men who wouldn't fit your pattern. And I'm wondering if the one you love now and say you want to marry really fits it better than anyone else. What *do* you want, Martha?'

'I was trying to tell you about Sam,' Martha answered. 'That I still care a great deal about him, whatever he thinks about me. There's something more human about him than any other man I've known. He isn't completely wrapped up in his work and his dreams, three quarters blind to the fact that anyone else exists at all.'

'Didn't you once think that he was?' Robina asked. 'I've a feeling that it's something you expect in a man, and even desire. I don't know why you should, unless it's to have a ready-made grievance. But if it isn't a thing that attracts you, how could you ever have fallen in love with Denis?'

Martha gave an odd laugh. 'So you've known that all along—that it's Denis?'

'No, I thought of it a little while ago. But it does make sense of several things, going all the way back to your New Year's party.'

'And so now you're going to try to make out that Denis is the murderer!'

'Well?' Robina said.

Martha moved swiftly towards her. She stood still just in front of her. She was inches taller than Robina, but she bent her head slightly, so that her face came close to Robina's. 'Haven't I told you he believes I'm a murderess? Haven't I told you he wouldn't do a thing to help me? Haven't I told you that now that Sam's been arrested I don't even trust him to keep his thoughts to himself? The truth is, he hardly cares about me at all. I love him, yes, and he let me think that he loved me, but I don't think he's really capable of loving anyone enough to do murder for them. That's where Sam's different. He could love or hate enough to murder. And so when I saw Douglas dead, and knew that he'd been to see him, and that it was my fault that he'd been to see him, and perhaps my fault that he'd killed him, as I believed he had, I decided to lie. I decided not to admit in any circumstances that I'd been here and seen what I had.'

'And you can't remember any of the details of the scene?' Robina asked. 'You can't remember if the book was on Douglas's knee, or the teacup on the floor, or even if the light was on?'

'I can't remember anything about the book or the cup.

The light . . .' Martha turned away and walked slowly back to the fireplace. 'I ought to remember the light. Was it on or did I turn it on? I ought to remember.' She stared straight before her, screwing her eyelids up a little as if in an effort to visualize the scene. After a moment she said in a low voice, 'I turned it on. I'm sure about that. The room was dark and—and I don't think the curtains were drawn. So you see—'

She turned sharply. She too had heard a sound from the hall. 'All right, Denis, come in,' she said. 'She knows all about you.'

The door opened and Inspector Morton came into the room.

CHAPTER 18

For a moment Martha was unable to speak.

Closing the door, Morton looked from her to Robina and said, 'That was an instructive conversation.'

Martha had recovered herself by then. 'How did you get in?' she asked furiously.

'The door was ajar,' Morton said. 'Didn't you know that?'

'No.'

'You didn't leave it open for Dr Ovenden?'

'No. And I don't think you found it open,' Martha said. 'I think you forced your way in somehow.'

'It was open all right,' he said.

Robina remembered how Martha had gone back to close the door properly after letting her in. It seemed clear now that what she had really gone back to do was to leave the door open so that Denis, whom she had been expecting, could get into the house and, hearing the voices in the drawing-room, disappear again without drawing attention to himself.

176

'Even if it was,' Martha said, 'what right have you simply to walk in and eavesdrop like that?'

'You people!' Morton said. 'Right! What right have you to keep to yourselves the things I've just heard you saying? A man's been murdered. It's not without a certain import- ance to find out who committed the murder. Or wouldn't you agree with that startling statement?'

'I thought you believed you knew who committed the murder,' Martha said. 'Anyone who knows Sam Mellanby could have told you you were wrong, but from the way you were acting it didn't seem likely that you'd listen.'

'So you decided not to make the effort to find out,' he said. 'I've just heard you making one of the most interesting statements that's been made since I started on this investi- gation, but learnt at the same time that you'd withheld it from me because it seemed to you that it was evidence against Dr Mellanby. You thought you were competent to judge a matter like that.' He made a sound of disgust. 'You clever people, taking on yourselves the right to give or withhold evidence that could take a man to the gallows, or save him from it!'

'That sounds very grand,' Martha said. 'I'd be more impressed by it if you hadn't already made the ridiculous mistake of arresting Sam Mellanby.'

She was being very grand herself. Robina could not help admiring her. To be caught out in a lie and perhaps in a serious position because of it did not seem to disturb Martha. She had, Robina thought, undoubtedly a great deal more courage than she allowed people to think.

Sitting down on a sofa, right in the middle of it, so that she looked enthroned there, and stretching out her arms along its back, Martha went on, 'If you'll tell me which of my statements it was that interested you so much, I'll do my best to repeat it.'

He gave her his hard-eyed stare, then turned to Robina. 'You made some interesting statements too, Mrs Mellanby.

177

And Dr Hillman's been to me with some interesting statements. A little late in the day, you're all allowing me to find out a few things. This deal he had on with Mr Birch, for instance, so that Mr Birch could take his wife to the United States. Quite an important point that, if you think it out, yet I've only just heard about it. And this matter of the ice in the tea. Couldn't you have given me that suggestion when I came to see you?'

'I hadn't thought of it then,' Robina said.

'But when you thought of it you came here with it instead of to me.' He turned back to Martha. 'Returning to your statement that you came to this house on the evening of your husband's murder, Mrs Birch, and found him dead, are you ready now to give me some more information about it?'

She inclined her head.

'You say that you found the room in darkness when you arrived,' he said.

'Yes.'

'And you switched on the light by the door?'

'Naturally.'

'And turned it off again when you left?'

She looked startled. 'I—I don't remember.'

'Try to remember.'

'I don't remember.'

'Think. You said just now that you took one look at the room and turned and ran. If that had happened, would you have thought of turning off the light?'

Martha's position had relaxed a little. She had brought her hands together in her lap. 'I might have,' she said. 'Automatically. But I don't remember it.'

'But you do remember turning on the light?'

'Yes.'

'Did you go into the room at all?'

'A step or two, perhaps.'

'No farther than that?'

'No. I was walking in and so I just went on walking, but only for a step or two.'

'You're sure you didn't go right in, feel in your husband's pockets for his wallet and take out the five hundred pounds that you knew would be there?'

Her hand flew to her mouth. She seemed to be locking in words ready to pour out. Then she let her hand drop again. 'No,' she said.

'You see, there are three possibilities about that money,' Morton said. 'Dr Mellanby, having just done the murder, may have taken it home with him and hidden it in the cupboard where the boy found it. Or the money may have been taken by someone else, who hid it in the Mellanbys' cupboard because she was afraid of carrying it around on her person and for the time being had nowhere else to hide it. I'm referring to you, of course, Mrs Birch. Or it may have been taken by someone who did not want it for himself, but who hid it in the Mellanbys' house as a way of helping to incriminate Dr Mellanby.'

'I didn't take it,' Martha said.

'But you did come here soon after five o'clock, find the room in darkness, switch on the light by the door, take one or two steps into the room, see the body of your husband, then turn and run?'

'Yes.'

'Possibly turning off the light, possibly not?'

'I think I did turn it off,' she said. 'I can't remember doing it, but I think I must have, because I do remember running down the passage in the darkness, and if that ceiling light in the room had been left on it would have shone down the passage, wouldn't it?'

'Turning it off, then. That's very interesting.'

'Why?' she asked uneasily.

'Because the only fingerprints on that switch were Miss Woods's.'

Martha looked down at her hands. She gave them a

puzzled, muddled stare, as if she could not imagine what strange property they possessed that prevented their leaving fingerprints behind them. 'I don't understand what you mean,' she said. 'How could that be?'

'It means,' Morton said, 'if you've told me the truth, that someone came into the room after you left and removed your prints from the switch. And that fits with what Mrs Mellanby suggested about the use that the ice was put to. It means that after you left someone went into your husband's room and carefully altered a good deal of the evidence so that what was left should point at Dr Mellanby.'

'But why?'

'Perhaps out of sheer hatred. Perhaps to protect you, having seen you come and go. Perhaps to protect himself. Have you considered that? Suppose you surprised the murderer, just after he'd committed his crime. Suppose he hid behind a curtain or a chair. If you came only a step or two into the room, and were stunned by shock, would you have been certain if there was anyone else in the room?'

'No.'

'But there's still another possibility. It may have seemed to this person, whoever it was, that any victim would be better than none. Suppose he came into the house, this unknown person, after you'd been here. Suppose he found your husband dead. And suppose that, although he'd seen Dr Mellanby come to the house, he hadn't seen you.'

'Well?'

'And suppose this person, for quite a while, had been making a nice thing out of blackmailing your husband. He sees at a glance that his income's stopped. He doesn't know who was responsible for stopping it, he hasn't the slightest idea who the murderer was, but he thinks he sees how he can set his income going again. He thinks all he has to do is change a little evidence, then go to Dr Mellanby and demand money. His experience with Douglas Birch has led him to believe that it's easy to blackmail people. He gets to work. He puts a book on Birch's knee, so that it should look as if he'd been reading when he was killed—but not knowing enough of your husband, or books in general, he chooses the one book your husband couldn't have been reading. He turns off the lamp by the chair on the other side of the fire, in which your husband would have been sitting if he'd really been reading. He pulls back the curtains. Now the scene's set so that it looks as if your husband had been reading by daylight. But there's still one thing wrong. After Mellanby left and before the murderer arrived, your husband had made some tea and the tea-pot's still hot. So this person does as Mrs Mellanby suggested to you just now—pours the hot tea away, takes some fresh tea, and puts ice in it to cool it down fast, putting the old tea leaves in a matchbox. Then he goes round, rubbing his fingerprints off anything that he might have touched, including the light by the door.'

Robina interrupted. 'But Ringrose was murdered himself!'

'He was,' Morton said.

'And you've just said that he did all those things because he *didn't* know who the murderer was. In that case there wasn't any motive for his murder.'

'Wasn't there?'

'What other motive could there have been, but that he knew too much?'

'Oh, he knew too much all right, but not about who murdered Douglas Birch,' Morton said.

'Aren't you forgetting something?' Martha said. 'I think you're forgetting what you yourself said just now, that the murderer could have been here when I came. Why shouldn't it have been the murderer who did all these things after I'd gone?'

'Because Ringrose did these things,' Morton said. 'Ringrose had the tea leaves in his pocket. Ringrose would have made the mistake about the book.'

'Then if he hadn't been murdered himself, wouldn't you

have thought that he was the murderer?' Martha asked. 'Perhaps he was, and was killed himself for some quite other reason.'

'No,' Morton said. 'So far as we know he couldn't have got hold of the hatchet, and so far as we know he had no motive for killing the man who was paying him handsomely for the simple service of keeping his mouth shut.'

'No one had a motive for killing Douglas!' Martha cried. 'No one had a real motive. Sam's couldn't seem real for a moment to anyone who knew him, and the same's true of mine, as I expect you heard me tell Mrs Mellanby.'

Morton nodded. 'I agree. None of the motives mentioned so far seem very real as one gets to know a little more of the people. And so I think the time's come . . .' He paused, then he wheeled suddenly towards the door. 'Yes, the time's come when I must have another talk with Dr Ovenden.'

Martha sprang up. As he reached for the door handle she thrust his hand aside and, slipping between him and the door, leant back against it. 'Why do you want to see him?' she demanded.

He stepped back a pace. 'Let me out, Mrs Birch,' he said.

'Why do you want to see Denis?'

'To ask for some more information about how he spent the afternoon when your husband was killed.'

'Do you suspect him of killing my husband and Harold Ringrose?'

'Let me out, please.'

'Do you suspect him?'

'I'm not going to answer that.'

'I insist on your telling me!'

He shook his head. 'The gesture's fine, but it would be simpler just to let me out without a fuss. I'm going to talk to Dr Ovenden. He gave Dr Mellanby an alibi which he's since admitted to be false. That leaves him without an alibi himself, unless he can tell me of anyone else who saw him that afternoon in the laboratory. Before going any further, I must find out if he can or not. Surely you can see that.'

She did not move away from the door. 'Denis had no motive for the murder of Ringrose,' she said. 'Even if he had one for the murder of my husband, even if you believe that, he had no reason to wish any harm to Ringrose.'

'Hadn't he?' Morton said in a level tone. 'Couldn't you say that Ringrose had prospered through Dr Ovenden's suffering?'

'But even if he did . . .'

'Let me out, Mrs Birch.' He reached out to thrust her aside. 'This is only wasting our time.'

Unwillingly she moved aside. He went out and they heard his quick steps crossing the hall, then the slam of the front door.

Martha dropped onto a chair and buried her face in her hands. Her shoulders began to quiver. 'He didn't do it,' she said in a choked whisper. 'Denis didn't do it.'

'You were expecting him to come here, weren't you?' Robina said. 'He hasn't come.'

Martha did not seem to hear her. 'If only I hadn't said Douglas was dead when I got here! If only I'd said I didn't see anything! They couldn't have proved it wasn't true.'

'Don't you believe Denis spent the afternoon in the lab?' Robina asked.

'I don't know, I don't know. How should I know?' Martha suddenly raised her head. 'No, he hasn't come,' she said, as if she had only just heard what Robina had said a moment earlier. 'I wonder why not? Before I left the Swinsons', I asked him to come, because I wanted to stop him looking at me as if I were a murderess and responsible for Sam's arrest. I couldn't talk to him when I was there, with everyone watching and listening. And he said he'd come—I think he said he'd come. But he isn't coming.' She dropped her head onto her hands again.

Robina went towards the door. 'I'll go home,' she said.

'If you don't like staying here by yourself and don't want to go back to the Swinsons', you can come with me.'

Martha did not answer. Robina was not sure that she had heard her, and repeated what she had said. Without looking up, Martha gave a shake of her head. Robina went out into the hall.

It was her intention as she did so to go straight home. She had a feeling that she almost ought to hurry, or Sam might reach home before her. She knew that this was absurd, that it would take longer than that, even if by now Morton was convinced that he had made a mistake about him. But still she felt that she must go quickly, as she might have felt if she had been going to meet a train, far too early, on which someone whom she loved was arriving, a feeling that by hurrying she might make time itself hurry up.

In spite of this, before she reached the door a thought checked her. She thought that she would look at the room in which Douglas had died. She had never seen it, but knew it only from Sam's description, a room at the end of the passage, a square room with a French window, a desk, two easy chairs, a lamp, and a sword hanging over the fireplace, a room that she would remember for the rest of her life.

Turning, she went swiftly along the passage. As she went she wondered if she would find the door locked, but it was not even quite closed. She pushed it open.

Even before she found the light switch she was aware of movement in the room. With her hand groping along the wall, she felt her heart racing in unreasoning panic. Then her fingers touched the switch and the light came on, the light that hung from the centre of the ceiling. She looked across the room.

'So you did come,' she said.

'Yes, I came,' Denis said.

He had been sitting in the chair that faced the window, but had got slowly to his feet as she came in. That was the movement that she had seen as the light from the passage behind her had entered the room. He stood before the empty fireplace, his heavy shoulders drooping, his hands hanging at his sides. His square face, that would have looked stolid but for the overbright, anxious eyes, was pasty with exhaustion and strain.

A curious thing happened in Robina then. Her mind seemed to split into two parts that had no communication with one another. In one part he was a murderer, of whom she was deadly frightened. The fear went prickling along her spine, almost paralysing her. But in the other part of her mind he was only Denis, who was Sam's friend and whom the children loved because of his own delight in them and because of the long, clever, patient games he played with them. It was to this Denis that she spoke, because she did not know how to speak to the other.

'When did you come?' she asked.

'Not long ago,' he said. 'I heard that policeman talking, so I came in here to wait. She's—she's still here, isn't she?'

'Martha? Yes. I don't think she knows you're here.'

He had looked away from her. His eyes could seldom meet the eyes of anyone else for long. So close a contact with another person was too much for him. 'I suppose you know all about it—us, I mean,' he said.

'I know a little about it,' she answered.

'I don't know how it happened,' he said. 'I didn't really want it to, but I didn't seem able to stop it.'

'That's happened to others before you. Denis—' She was looking round the room, taking in the way the chairs were arranged, seeing the lamp beside the chair in which Denis had been sitting, the window behind the other. She looked too at the sword that hung on the wall behind Denis's head, the sword with which Douglas had chased Martha out into the darkness, shouting after her threats that he would use it. How preposterous that sounded, how impossible. But Miss Woods had heard it. It had happened. 'Denis, did you come here that afternoon?'

He said confusedly, 'That afternoon?'

'When Douglas was killed. When you were supposed to be in the lab.'

'I *was* in the lab,' he said.

Inspector Morton's looking for you to ask you that,' she said. 'Can you prove it?'

'I don't know.'

'Didn't you see anyone? Didn't anyone come in and talk to you?'

'I—I'm not sure. I haven't thought about it.'

'Think about it now,' she said.

He looked at her again and this time his eyes held hers in an intent stare. 'Do they believe I did it, Robina? Is that what they think now?'

'Did you, Denis?'

'I only wish I had!' he answered.

It was spoken with an intensity that Robina had never heard from Denis before. It made her remember what Iris had said of him, of his temper, his white-faced, silent rages.

He went on, 'It would make it so much simpler. I should know what to do. And I might have done it. I had reason, hadn't I? Douglas wouldn't let Martha go—that's a reason that would convince everybody. That's the way it could have been, if only I'd thought of it. I could have said, when they came to question me, that I hadn't been in the lab—'

'Denis, what are you talking about?' Robina asked sharply.

'About a way out. I'm going mad, not knowing what to do, and I've got to find a way out.'

From behind Robina, Martha said, 'Isn't there only one way out for you, Denis?' She had come silently into the room. She walked past Robina and went close to Denis, looking into his face. She was almost as tall as he was and was holding herself very erect. Her beauty, that had seemed almost dead only a little while before, had kindled again, shining in her white face with a desperate radiance. 'My car's outside,' she said. 'Isn't that the simplest thing? Here are the keys.'

He started to tremble. But at the same time he smiled. 'You think I'd do anything for you, don't you—anything?' he said.

'You like things simple,' she said. 'You always said so.'

'Yes, and so I wanted you to leave Douglas and come away with me,' he said. 'I wanted a simple and honest love between us. And I've only found out today why you wouldn't come.'

'It would have ruined you,' she said. 'That's why I wouldn't.'

'Oh no,' he said. 'Oh no.'

Robina could see that he wanted to say more, but that he was shaking so that he could not speak.

'You'd never have gone on loving me if I'd come between you and your work,' Martha said. 'I always knew that. But I never thought—I never dreamt—that you wanted me so much that you'd—that you'd actually . . .'

'That I'd do murder?' He raised his hands suddenly and grasped her shoulders, close to the base of her throat. 'Stop it, Martha! You're making it too simple for me—d'you understand that? You're making it too simple.'

Robina had taken a step forward. But then she stood still again. As if they could not help themselves, her eyes left Denis's distorted face and Martha's white mask and fastened onto the sword hanging on the wall.

'The sword,' she said. 'Of course, it wasn't the sword!'

The words startled both of them. Denis dropped his hands. Martha turned slowly, one of her hands going to her throat.

'We all thought it was the sword that Douglas threatened to use against you, Martha,' Robina said. 'But of course it wasn't. He had another weapon. All these months there's been another weapon that he's held over your head. Because it was you who killed Booker, wasn't it? It was you who took the car out after the party and ran Booker down and left him in the ditch to die.'

Martha stepped swiftly backwards. She looked from Robina to Denis, then back to Robina. 'It was Douglas,' Martha said.

'No,' Robina said. 'If it had been, you could have left him, you would have left him. That's what Denis understood today, when he heard that Douglas had been paying blackmail and that you'd said it was for the death of Booker. Denis saw then that Douglas had been paying blackmail for you and that he could hold that over you, threatening to take his knowledge of you to the police if you tried to leave him. And you knew that he meant it and that as long as he wanted he could prevent your having your freedom. That's why you killed him. And it's why you killed Ringrose—not because you thought he knew you'd killed Douglas, but because you thought he knew you'd killed Booker. I remember Edna telling us how upset you were when you heard that Douglas had been paying blackmail. Perhaps it was only then that you found that he knew about you.'

'You said yourself I couldn't have killed Douglas,' Martha said. 'You said so only a little while ago.'

'Because I thought you hadn't time,' Robina said. 'I didn't understand that all the things in this room, the lights, the curtains, the tea, had been arranged by Ringrose. You did have time—just to come here, hit Douglas in the head, grab the money and run straight back. And I thought you hadn't a real motive. I thought you could leave Douglas whenever you really wanted to. Denis knows all this is true.'

'I've known it since yesterday,' he said. 'All this time she said she loved me, but she let me take the blame for that . . . She never even asked me to do it for her. She let me think she half believed I'd done it. If she'd asked me I shouldn't have cared, I'd have done anything, but she never even asked me . . .'

Martha turned to him again. For a moment there was an

agony of supplication in her look, then it changed to fierce anger. 'You never loved me!' she cried. 'You were like the others, you hated me, you always hated me! I'd kill you too if I could!'

Suddenly she made for the door. With incredible swiftness she ran down the passage. Robina started after her but collided with Denis in the doorway. Drawing back, she saw his face and, instead of hurrying on, put her hand on his arm. Together they went along the passage.

As they reached the front door, which was standing wide open, they saw the headlights of a car sweep across the front of the house. Dimmed by the dense fog, they glowed dull orange, scarcely lighting up a couple of yards in front of the car as it accelerated crazily down the drive.

'The gates!' Robina screamed and started to run again. 'She's forgotten the gates are locked!'

She was jerked back by Denis, who had her fast by the shoulder. His grip hurt her and sent the vibration of his trembling into her arm. He stood quite still until they heard the sound of the crash. Then he let Robina go and went staggering back into the empty house.

CHAPTER 19

The wardrobe had been destroyed. That had been almost the first thing that Sam had done after he returned home. Standing in the hall, still with his arms round Robina and with Miles and Miranda holding onto such parts of him as they could reach, and Mrs Booker looking on a little tearfully from the kitchen doorway, he had said that until they had got rid of the horrible thing they could not even start to forget the last few days.

Working in the garden in the light that fell from the open kitchen door, Sam had sawed the wardrobe into little pieces.

The children, who were inclined to believe that this was a sort of exorcism of the three-footed witch, had joined ecstatically in the destruction. To be allowed to smash something so great, so apparently sure of itself as a whole wardrobe, was almost too good to be true.

But to have made the evening perfect for them, it would have been necessary to make a bonfire of all the pieces there and then, and this Sam and Robina refused to do. Not that they would have minded burning up such a useful supply of firewood in one great blaze, but it would be, they both said, too conspicuous and not really the right thing to do at the moment. They obtained peace by a promise that there would be a bonfire someday.

Going indoors again, with enough wood to start the sitting-room fire, they saw Miles and Miranda eying certain pieces of furniture with a new interest, and saw that it would have to be made clear that the events of this evening were not to be considered a precedent.

Mrs Booker swept up the hall after the wardrobe had gone, then came to say goodbye.

'Now you're almost straight, you'll only be wanting me the days we arranged,' she said, 'so I'll come next Tuesday. You'll like it when you're settled. I've lived here twenty-seven years and I like it all right. Some people say you don't get much life here and they'd sooner live in Blanebury, but I like it all right. Of course I miss my little fellow. It's nice to have a man to fix things and he used to give me a lot of laughs—I'll always miss him. But after a time you stop thinking about the death, you know, and it don't seem to matter that much who done it, the poor soul. I didn't know I felt like that exactly, but—' She shrugged her shoulders and tightened her scarf under her chin. 'I'll be along Tuesday,' she said.

When she had gone Sam and Robina put the children to bed. It had to be allowed to take a long time, and then Sam had to read aloud for a long time, with Robina staying to listen. Both children had felt instinctively that tonight they had special privileges, and naturally exploited them to the utmost. But at last they got too sleepy to listen any more, and let themselves be given good night kisses. The light was turned out and Sam and Robina went downstairs.

'I've got a confession to make,' Robina said as they reached the sitting-room. 'I don't think there's anything to eat.'

'Nothing?' Sam said aghast. 'Nothing at all?'

'Oh, there are eggs. The trouble was I was expecting that nice butcher's boy to bring a joint. I suppose he didn't come because he was a little unwilling to deliver meat to a murderer's household, but I'd put the whole thing out of my mind and forgot I ought to go out and get something else.'

'Well, what's the matter with eggs?' Sam put an arm round her. 'You had certain other things on your mind too. Anyway, let's not bother about it yet.'

'All right,' Robina said, 'let's just sit and talk for a while.'

'Or not talk,' Sam said.

They sat down together by the fire. Robina's hair, which had started the day done up so carefully, had bit by bit been coming more adrift. Sam, thrusting a hand through it, encountered one or two remaining hairpins and shook them out.

'That's better,' he said as her hair fell about her small, sharp-featured face. 'That's back to normal.'

'What d'you think, Sam?' she said. 'Should I have a perm for a change? I always had it at one time, but it got so expensive. Would you like it, d'you think?'

'I might,' he said.

'You'd like me to bother about those things more than I do, wouldn't you?'

He laughed and kissed her. 'It's *your* hair.'

'Well, I'll think about it. Sam . . .'

'I know,' he said. 'Go on. We've got to talk about it a bit.'

'Just a little. It's about Denis. What's going to happen to him now?'

'From the sound of things, a bit of a breakdown.'

'Will he have to leave here?'

'I don't see why. He's got Edna to look after him. You couldn't find anyone better. And Pete will be good sort of company. And Iris . . . What d'you think about Iris?'

'I think he's lost her irrevocably to Pete, if Pete wants her, and I think, rather to his surprise, he probably does.'

'That'll be far better for her.'

'Sam . . .' She pushed her hair back behind her ears, drew her knees up and dug her chin into them. 'What was the truth about those two—Martha and Denis? And what really happened at that party?'

'You're meaning the scene Denis made and the way he got drunk?'

'Yes. Was he in love with Martha then? Was that what it was all about?'

'I suppose so. He'd been going around mostly with Iris until then, but they had some sort of a row on the day of the party and she didn't go. Don't you think that's what it was about? She'd somehow found out about Martha.'

'When she told me yesterday about the quarrel she didn't say so.'

'That could be a sort of loyalty, or a sort of pride.'

'And you think she's known all this time about Martha?'

'I rather think so. She's been very nervy and difficult for a long time, not at all like she used to be. And it would explain why she made the scene she did over Pete the other night. Probably she had a sort of feeling that Martha could take any man she wanted away from her. She thought Martha wanted him.'

'As you and I did.'

'Yes.'

'But in fact, when we thought that, she'd just come from killing Douglas.'

He stroked her arm. 'Do we have to go on?'

'There's just one thing more. When she went over there, taking the hatchet with her, she couldn't have known she was going to kill Douglas, could she? She couldn't even have known that he'd be in. Then why did she take the hatchet?'

'I suppose to protect herself, in case he was in and came after her again with the sword. She probably was really afraid of him. And then when she saw him sitting there quietly and saw that she'd a wonderful opportunity to kill him, she couldn't resist it.'

'And the money? Did she leave it here to make trouble for you, or just because she'd nowhere else to hide it?'

'Does it matter which? If the wood hadn't arrived when it did she might have got away with it all. And I might not be sitting here now.'

'D'you really think that? I don't. I think Inspector Morton would have got at the truth somehow.'

'D'you know,' Sam said thoughtfully, 'I'm not absolutely certain that I share your enthusiasm for Inspector Morton. I found something distinctly unsympathetic in his personality. Besides, I've been hearing altogether too much about him from you for the last hour or two.'

'I have a great respect for him—' She broke off at the sound of violent knocking on the front door.

Sam clasped her to him. 'Don't go!' he said. 'Every time there's been knocking like that at that door during the last few days it's meant trouble. Don't go!'

She disentangled herself and stood up. 'It might be the inspector,' she said.

'If it is,' Sam said 'I'm out. You're out. The children are out. There's no one at home at all.'

Laughing, she went to the door. Outside she saw a boy with round cheeks and red hair. He thrust a package rolled up in newspaper into her hands.

'It's the beef,' he said. 'Sorry I didn't get along with it sooner, but with this fog I got all behind in my deliveries. You know—"Season of mists and mellow fruitfulness!" Nearly didn't get round to you at all. Any orders for next week, Mrs Mellanby?'

'Next week,' Robina said. 'Yes, I suppose I'd better start thinking about next week.'

>>> If you've enjoyed this book and would like to discover more great vintage crime and thriller titles, as well as the most exciting crime and thriller authors writing today, visit: >>>

The Murder Room
Where Criminal Minds Meet

themurderroom.com